FROM USA TODAY BESTSELLING AUTHOR

ERIN BEDFORD

PROTECTED BY THE Vampires

HOUSE OF DURAND
BOOK THREE

Protected by the Vampires © 2019
Embrace the Fantasy Publishing, LLC

Also by Erin Bedford

Curse of the Fairy Tales
Rapunzel Untamed
Rapunzel Unveiled

Her Angels
Heaven's Embrace
Heaven's A Beach
Heaven's Most Wanted

House of Durand
Indebted to the Vampires
Wanted by the Vampires
Protected by the Vampires

Academy of Witches
Witching On A Star
As You Witch
Witch You Were Here
Just Witch It
Summer Witchin'

Granting Her Wish
Vampire CEO

FROM USA TODAY BESTSELLING AUTHOR

ERIN BEDFORD

PROTECTED
BY THE Vampires

HOUSE OF DURAND
BOOK THREE

Chapter 1
Piper

IF ANYONE HAD TOLD me last year, that I would be standing here in front of an expansive mansion that looked like it had forgotten it wasn't the fifteenth century anymore, I would have laughed in their faces.

The reddish grey stone of the mansion decorated every inch of the exterior, including the little fence that wrapped around the backyard. Large white windows filled the walls of all three stories. There were pointed metal weathervanes on the tops of the darker grey shingled roof and an actual tower on one side of the mansion. However, none of that compared to the large set of double doors looming before us like a vortex of doom waiting to suck us in and never let go.

I shifted in my seat in the limo as it pulled up to the entryway along a gravel drive. The double doors swung open just as we parked, and a severe looking man stepped out. He reminded me of Darren the first time I met him—stern demeanor, no emotion in his eyes, and every piece of clothing perfectly in place. Except unlike Darren, who was every woman's fantasy butler, this guy was old. Like, ancient old. Mummies had better skin than this guy.

"Who's that?" I murmured to no one in particular, as I stared out the tinted windows. The six men—vampires—in the back of the limo were tense and quiet as we prepared to leave the confines of the vehicle. It wasn't until I asked my question that they broke their silence.

"That is the housekeeper, Fauns. Think of him as Darren, but less..." Wynn smirked. "Fun." Wynn tilted his head to the side, watching with amusement as his ebony hair fell into his face, covering those gorgeous blues for a second. Wynn always had a laid-back, carefree kind of air about him, but today was different. While he put on his usual persona, today it was forced. There was a tightness to his jaw that wasn't there before, and believe me, I watched him enough to know. It made me nervous for what was about to happen.

My eyes shifted over to Antoine. By all accounts, now that I was his human servant, he could feel my apprehension. But, if he did, the head of the Durand house didn't show it. He was perfectly at ease, bored almost, and ready to get this over and done with.

As if feeling my eyes on him, Antoine's shifted from the window to meet mine. Those pale, almost white blue eyes watched me with interest. The bite on my neck pulsated and my hand immediately went there. His eyes followed, filling with heat that made me blush and press my thighs together. There was a subtle shift in the other occupants of the car and a deep inhale, before a collective set of groans filled the backseat.

"Let me out before I bust a nut in here," Drake growled, his large form pushing through the others and shoving the limo door open before Darren could open it.

While we had left just after dusk, it was almost dawn now, and the sky had lightened considerably. My masters were no doubt happy for it, since light was no friend of theirs.

Vampires. I huffed a laugh to myself. Talk about things I'd never have believed. If the mansion was impossible, then the men exiting the limo like the devil himself was on their heels were improbable. However improbable though, I couldn't imagine going back to my life before. I couldn't bear it.

Fauns stood outside by the limo door, waiting with an umbrella over his head as if he were expecting rain.

"Me too." Rayne crawled out of the car next, but not before moving those amber eyes over me once more. There was hurt and confusion in his gaze. I wanted to wrap my arms around the youngest of the vampire brothers and make him understand my choice.

There really hadn't been a choice at all. I hadn't wanted to become anyone's human servant, and yet here I was, bitten and wondering what the hell I had been thinking.

Still, I hadn't picked Antoine to hurt Rayne or any of the others. I was being practical for once in my goddamn life. It came down to one big reason really.

Valentine scared me.

Antoine scared Valentine.

Hence, Antoine had to be the one to do it. It was as simple as that. Still, even if I had all the best reasons in the world, I didn't think it would make Rayne hurt any less. At least the others seemed to be taking it rather well, or as far as I could tell. They weren't big on showing their hands to anyone, least of all to me.

"Piper." Wynn's voice jerked me out of my thoughts and I realized I was the last one in the vehicle. Wynn had waited behind and was offering me his hand. With a small, shaky smile, I slipped mine into his cool grasp.

Pulling me from the car, Wynn wrapped an arm around my waist and lowered his mouth to my ear. "How are you feeling?"

I hummed and glanced away from the looming mansion to meet his gaze. How was I feeling? I had pushed my feelings to the back of my mind because of what waited for us here in Washington. Back on the plane, though, it had been a blur of anxiety and excitement, and then there was the mixture of pain and pleasure. Then...nothing. After I woke up, we'd been

11

ready to get off the plane and head to the house. I hadn't had much of a chance to assess how I felt.

If I was being honest, I expected...more. Like, superpowers or something. It was silly, I guess, to expect to suddenly have super strength or I don't know...something.

I did feel different sure. Not like I expected though. It was like I'd had the best sleep of my life and was hyped up on a triple shot of espresso. I could *feel* so much more than before. The colors were brighter, the sounds...louder, and even the air tasted different. Not better, per se, but I could point out different scents unlike before. Kind of gross honestly.

For example, the limo.

Pre-biting—PB for short—I would have just said it had a clean smell to it. Like sheets fresh out of the dryer. But now...I could tell that someone had smoked in the back at one point in time. Another person had spilled some kind of alcohol on the back seat...and there was just a subtle scent of musk and sweat. I didn't want to think too much about what that was from. Part of me shuddered just thinking about it.

"Cold?" Wynn asked, dropping his arm with a frown. "Sorry, I forget sometimes."

I shook my head and offered him a smile. "No, it's not you. And for how I'm feeling, okay, I guess. Overwhelmed. Wondering why Antoine is being a dick and if Rayne will ever forgive me."

Rayne, who stood by the front door with the twins, stiffened. His shoulders bunching up to his ears. I could see the strain he was under as he tried not to turn around. I knew he'd hear me talking to Wynn, it was hard to keep anything a secret around this bunch. Hopefully, that meant he knew how badly I felt about it all.

Wynn gave me a lopsided grin as we walked up the steps to join them. "Don't worry too much about it, lovely. There are worse things, believe me."

Allister moved in next to us and jerked his head towards the open door. "And most of those are inside this house."

"Ain't that the truth," Drake scoffed.

I was happy to have the twins so close. While all six of the guys were vampires, only Marcus, Drake, and Allister really had that 'I will protect you from the world itself' kind of build to them. Large and muscled in all the right places, they could

13

give those men on the front of romance novels a run for their money. I'd be happy to let them rip my bodice any time.

Rayne snorted.

My eyes shot to him where his nose crinkled up and a small smile tugged at his lips. His red hair was pulled back with a clip, so his face was easily seen. His amber eyes twinkled with amusement and the freckles along the bridge of his nose stood out sharply against his pale skin. It made his face look older, more mature, like he might actually be several decades old and not barely younger than me. In vampire years, Rayne was still a baby, but it was me who was the baby of the bunch. I was pushing thirty and surrounded by younger faces and older souls. How did this happen to me?

My thoughts of my own existence were pushed to the side as the men around me stiffened. Even Darren, who was usually so unaffected by things, had a caution to him. As if we were gazelle who had heard a stick break, we froze, except that stick was the soft, almost nonexistent footsteps of a man. Not a man. A vampire.

The six vampires I lived with were the Hollywood version of vampires—the dark lovers of their species—gorgeous and more interested in what was between my legs than in my veins. But the man—if you could call him that—who walked toward us, with the stunning Theresa just behind him, was something out of the horror films.

About my height at five-foot-five, and with a balding head and large ears, his face was pinched, and his lips were contorted in an almost permanent snarl. His fangs weren't the only sharp things in his mouth. Every single tooth was pointed and when he grinned, it was like staring into the face of a shark. Shudder inducing for sure.

The rest of him was just as unappealing in nature. He wore an old double-breasted suit with a fluffy undershirt, and sleeves that peeked out of the cuffs. He was mismatched in his ancient style standing next to Theresa's modern chic. Her long, dark hair was pulled up off her neck and into a twisted updo. The skintight dress I'd seen her in last had been replaced with a red formfitting sheathe that reached to just above her knee and plunged in the front, stopping just before her naval. I envied her style, but not her residence. I didn't know how she could stand being near him, let alone live in the same house as him.

Her master's hand moved out from behind her waist and I applauded her for not sighing in relief. Those hands were thin and sharp, with a long nail on the end of each finger. He waved one of those hands in our direction, and for a moment I was confused.

A hand pulled me down to my knees. Wincing at the sudden impact to my joints, my eyes jerked to Allister who had dropped me, and then I noticed all the others had genuflected as well. Even Marcus—someone I couldn't imagine bowing to anyone—sat on the ground before this monstrous man.

"Master," Antoine greeted, propped up on one knee before the man. "Thank you for having us in your home."

The master vampire barked a laugh and waved a hand at us. "Yes, yes. Of course. Get up already, Antoine. Humble does not suit you. Nor do I believe it for one second."

Antoine didn't show any reaction, except for the slight stiffening in his shoulders as he stood. The rest of us apparently had leave to stand as well, because the others moved from their feet and Allister helped me on to mine. I kept hold of his hand, squeezing it tightly with my small fingers. Allister's blue green eyes darted down to me for a moment, but he didn't release my hand.

The master moved around our group, taking in each of us before muttering something or another for that person to hear, making their shoulders bunch and tension rise. For once, I was happy I didn't have vampire hearing.

"Darren, my boy." The master clapped Darren on the shoulder like he was a much beloved grandson that he never got to see. "I see you are still as ripe and succulent as the day you joined my Antoine's service. Glad to see the life hasn't been completely drained from you...yet."

Yikes. Make that a creepy ass uncle.

Darren took it all in stride of course, nodding his head slightly, leaving his dark eyes locked on the ground. Even though we weren't at home, he still wore a suit and tie, as well as his white gloves. His black hair was slicked back from his handsome face, but it was all a mask. I'd figured that out now. He hid behind his perfection like an armor against the two worlds he was straddling. I guess I was straddling them now as well. With one leg in the human world and one in the vampire world, neither one of us would ever be able to fully belong to either one.

For a second, my heart raced as I realized that my existence had been changed forever. Just like Darren, I wouldn't age. I would stay exactly as I was forever and ever. No wrinkles. No grey hairs. I'd never become an old woman sitting on her porch surrounded by my grandbabies. Well, I guess I could still have grandbabies and kids, as far as anyone has told me my own body hadn't changed that much.

"And who is this lovely morsel?" The raspy voice stopped before me and I realized it was me that was the lovely morsel. Like I was some piece of candy and not a human being.

I glanced to Antoine for some kind of guidance, but he didn't even turn his eyes my way. Bastard. Flipping my attention back to the vampire before me, I watched as he lifted my hands in his worn and wrinkled ones. He brought them up to his face, and for a moment I thought he might kiss them, but then he...sniffed me. A long inhale that shivered through him and made me want to gag.

"Ah, yes. I can see why Valentine is so taken with her. She is a rare beauty." The master lifted his gaze to mine. I gasped, making him smile. His eyes. They were red. Not a brown like I'd thought before, but actually red, like dry blood on the floor. It made him even more frightening than before.

I swallowed hard and tried to still my racing heart.

"Do not fear me, child. All react to me this way the first time." He reached a hand up and cupped the side of my face, his long nails so close to my eye that I had to force myself not to flinch. "And what is your name, precious?"

I was pretty sure he knew my name. I didn't know what game he was playing, but two could play that game. Licking my dry lips, I said the first thing that came to my mind. "Yours first."

The men around me stiffened, and even Theresa frowned at my words, but the ancient vampire simply threw his head back and laughed. "Yes, yes. That fire. That energy. I bet she tastes divine. Doesn't she, Antoine?"

Antoine froze but then answered, "I do not know what you mean, master."

The vampire clucked his tongue but turned his eyes back to me. "You should know by now not to lie to me, lad. I see as well as smell your mark on her. You've made her yours as well? Now, aren't we a greedy boy. No wonder you turned down Valentine's offer to buy her." The way he chastised Antoine made my stomach roll and I wanted nothing more than to be back home. I knew the likelihood of that happening was about as likely as Darren letting anyone muss his perfect hair.

Those blood-red eyes focused on me as the master scanned over my form. "Yes, I can quite see how you would have all of my boys in such a tizzy."

"I don't," Theresa scoffed. Her arms crossed over her chest, making her dress shift enough to show more of her breasts. "She is positively...common."

Before I even realized he had moved, Theresa's head snapped to the side and blood trickled from the edge of her lips. "When I want your opinion, Theresa, I will ask for it."

"Yes, master." Theresa bowed her head, not bothering to wipe the blood from her mouth.

"Now...where were we?" The master gave a small smile before taking a step back from me. I flinched as he bowed low at the waist, his hand coming out in front of him to brush the floor. "I, my delicious peach, am Count Boris Stravinsky. Master of this...ragtag bunch." He flashed his fangs as he tossed a hand at the men around me. "Now, I have told you my name..." He trailed off, holding his hand out to me.

Licking my lips, I cleared my throat. "Piper. Piper Billings." I frowned and then gave a clumsy curtsy that had me losing my balance. Allister's hand caught me before I fell over and made an even bigger fool of myself.

Boris laughed loudly at my misstep. "You, my dear, are a delight. I cannot wait to see what this week brings. Come, come. Let me show you around my home." The men around me stiffened as Boris wrapped his arm around my shoulders and directed me toward the hallway.

"Oh, calm yourselves." Boris scowled at the fretting vampires. "I will bring your servant back in one piece. In fact, one of you may accompany us." He stopped us and turned to wait for the six men, lingering where I had stood.

For a moment, nobody moved, and then Darren, ever the responsible one, announced, "I will take the bags to our rooms." He inclined his head and bowed slightly with one gloved hand to his heart, first to Boris and then to Antoine.

See? Why couldn't I be that poised? He knew exactly what to do and when to do it. He even knew to acknowledge Boris first!

It was Boris, not Antoine, who waved Darren off, showing that even though Darren belonged to Antoine, Boris had say over everyone. All those wonderful walls I thought we'd built around me started to crumble. So much for being safe.

I watched the men before me, my face frozen in a polite smile. I hoped my eyes screamed how much I needed someone by my side. It wasn't Antoine who answered my call, the one who should have since he was supposed to be able to feel my emotions, but Marcus. The large vampire stepped forward, his face set in a blank expression.

"Ah, Marcus. Yes, good. Good. You will accompany us." Boris patted Marcus on the arm, a move that would have made me flinch, but either they were used to Boris's overfamiliar actions or they feared him too much to show their discomfort.

With the way the other's faces melted into a mixture of concern as we walked away, I had a feeling it was the latter.

Chapter 2
Wynn

THE MOMENT OUR MASTER left the room, Theresa's eyes were locked on me like a huntress finally finding her prey, as she sashayed in my direction. God, you'd think the woman would take a hint.

"Wynn," she purred, her hands coming up to my chest as she pouted her lips at me. "I'm so happy to see you back in our glorious home." I rolled my eyes over her shoulder at Drake, who only smirked at me before shaking his head and heading upstairs. His counterpart followed after him, taking the stairs two at a time.

Antoine's phone rang and he answered it, speaking in French as he made his way into the den rather than upstairs. Rayne was the only one left behind with me, but one look in his direction told me he wasn't going to be any help. His eyes were focused on where Piper had disappeared with our master, and he had no time for me and my problems.

It didn't keep me from trying though. *A little help here.*

Rayne's gaze reluctantly turned from the hallway to me. He scanned over Theresa, who was now plastered all over my front, and arched a brow. With a smirk and a chuckle, he headed for the stairs, shaking his head the whole way up.

Fucking twat. I shoved the thought in his direction, gaining me an even louder laugh from him. Holding back a scowl and a sigh, I redirected my attention to the woman in my arms. The crazy woman with a tendency to lash out at anyone who stood in her way. Thankfully, since our master had taken Piper, she was well and out of her mind. For now, at least.

"Come now, Wynn." Theresa pouted, pulling the clip out of her hair so the long, curly tresses fell around her shoulders

25

like a waterfall. She sure knew how to work her assets. "Don't pretend like you didn't miss me even a little bit. Don't we have fun together?"

I lifted my eyes to the ceiling and drew my arm around her waist. "Theresa, lovely, you are a gorgeous woman, but you know I'm a free spirit. I won't be—"

"Bound to one woman. I know. I know." Theresa sighed and then rolled her eyes with a giggle. "I'm not proposing marriage. I just want to reminisce. You know, about the good old days?" Her hand trailed down my silk shirt and played along the line of my pants before cupping me in her hand. I grunted and let her fondle me for a moment, though I'd rather have anyone else's hands on me than the viper holding my family jewels.

"Theresa," I started, trying again and pushing her hand away. "We're in the foyer."

Theresa gave me a sly smile. "That's never stopped you before."

Completely dropping my arm away from her and stepping back, I tucked my hands into my pockets and frowned at her. "That was before. When I had to do as our master bid. As you do."

She scoffed and tossed her hair over her shoulder. "Don't act like you were forced, Wynn. You enjoyed all the women and men our master provided you."

I gave her a small push as I stepped back. "That was then."

Theresa gave me an amused smirk. "And you've changed? Since when? I remember not too long ago," she moved in closer once more and walked her fingers up my chest, "when you were more than happy to spend some time with me."

I gave her a lopsided grin but then moved out of her reach once more. "Things are different now." I couldn't help but let my eyes stray to where Piper had disappeared. Theresa noticed.

"Because of her? The human?" She barked a laugh but when I didn't laugh with her, she dropped her hands and frowned. "You can't be serious? She's human and Antoine's servant. She doesn't even belong to you."

I shrugged a shoulder. "That's my problem. Not yours."

For a second, something flashed behind her eyes. Worry. Fear. But it was gone in an instant and a seductive smile spread across her ruby red lips once more. With a secretive look around, she pressed her chest against mine, her mouth touching my ear. To any passing human, it would look like she was whispering naughty secrets into my ear, but a vampire would know the truth. What she really said was, "Come with me, you're all in danger."

A smarter man wouldn't have allowed Theresa to lead him into the drawing room where she pushed me onto the couch and closed the sliding doors behind her. A different man would have seen her caution as a pretense to get me alone and have her wicked way with me. However, Theresa wasn't human. She also didn't believe in pretenses or lies. She was upfront with what she wanted and made damn well sure you knew it. Which was why, when she said we were in danger, I believed her.

Theresa sashayed over to me, placing one high heel on the couch next to me so that the skirt she wore split at the opening, showing me all her ivory skin and that she wasn't wearing anything beneath it. Theresa played with the line of her neckline as if to tease me with a peek of her breast, but her mouth was saying something different.

"You shouldn't have come here." Her words were low and seductive, a glaring contradiction to her actions.

I stared up at her, placing a hand on her ankle but not moving it higher. "And how do you suggest we say no? We'd lose our heads while we were sleeping...if we were lucky."

Theresa's brows furrowed for a second before she continued the charade, untying the strings of her dress slowly, but my eyes remained on her face the whole time. "It's a trap. Master doesn't like what Valentine reported. He thinks you have become too mainstream." She dropped the ties, releasing her breasts to the room. My eyes didn't even dip.

"Then why invite us home? Why not kill us already?" I leaned forward so my hand trailed up her calf. If anyone walked into the room, they'd see us and think we were about to fuck. Which was the point. There were far more humans than vampires in this house. Most of the vampires were already out on the hunt, looking for their evening meal. The humans, however, would be finishing up their chores for the day and their human sensibilities demanded them to turn around and leave a room if someone was in our position. Still, we had to be careful.

"Because of the girl," Theresa explained, climbing into my lap so her breasts were pressed up against my chest, with my hands curled around her waist. "Valentine wants her."

I let out a low growl, my fingers digging into her sides. "He can't have her."

Theresa gave me a wry smile. "A lesser woman would be jealous that such a human has captivated your whole house. However, her life is fleeting, but yours is not. Give them the girl and they will make sure you go home to your home in that pitiful town of yours. Refuse, and they will make you pay."

My fangs flashed at her as I flipped us, tossing her onto the couch as I snarled above her. "What is he planning? What's the game?"

Theresa didn't seem worried, even when my hand latched around her throat. I should have known better than to threaten her with violence, she got off on it. Hell, it was her kink, something I'd been more than happy to oblige her with before. That was then. Now, it just pissed me off.

I pushed off her and scoffed as I dragged my hand through my hair. "We won't give her up. He can't make us."

Theresa sat up on her elbow, not bothered by her nakedness as she shrugged. "Then she'll die. Or you will. Depends on the master's mood really. Though..." She smiled and giggled. "The way he's acting, he might just take her for himself. You know how much he likes to break little things like her. Even more so than Valentine. You'd be better off killing her yourself."

I hated to admit it, but she was right. Valentine was the way he was for a reason. Our master had particular tastes as well, and while those tastes didn't always line up with females, for the right one and the right reason, our master would make an exception.

Shit.

"What are you going to do?" Theresa watched me as I paced the room, my thoughts going a thousand miles a minute. I shot her a look, which made her sit up on the couch. "You are seriously considering defying him, aren't you? She's not worth it." Theresa wrapped the straps of her dress back around her neck and stood. "No human is worth it. Believe

31

me. She'll get tired of it—of you—and before you know it, she'll resent you for making her immortal. If you think she loves you now, you're only making it possible for her to hate you later." Theresa crossed her arms over her chest stared hard at me. "Take it from someone who knows."

Theresa did know. She wasn't much older than me. We'd both been created around the same time. She was one of our master's exceptions. Most of his children were men, except for a couple of others. They were all as twisted as Theresa was. But he made a mistake when creating Theresa.

She'd been married. Something he hadn't bothered to check before changing her. All our master saw was a beautiful creature who loved to cause pain almost as much as she liked to receive it. It was a rare thing for someone of her breeding back then. A duchess, I believe. When our master changed her, she wanted to bring her husband along with her. She loved him and couldn't bear to leave him behind, but our master forbid her to change him into a vampire. I didn't remember why, but Theresa defied him anyway and made the duke into a human servant.

"What happened to Jean Paul?" I asked after a few moments of silence. "Did you kill him, or did he do it himself?"

The smile on her lips was bitter and sad. "Neither. It was Valentine who did the deed." I took a step toward her, but she held up her hand, stopping me. "He said he was saving me the trouble since Jean Paul had decided to confess his sins to a priest before taking his own life." She let out a long sigh as she played with the ends of her hair. "Valentine caught him coming out of the church right after sunset. They had to burn the whole perish to the ground just to ensure they told no one else of our existence." She laughed dryly. "It's ironic really. Why confess your sins before committing the most unforgivable sin? I guess he thought hell would have been better than being with me forever."

"Theresa," I started, but the door to the drawing room opened, revealing Valentine himself. Dressed in a modern suit and tie, Valentine's long hair was tied back at the nape of his neck. His watchful eyes widened slightly at the sight of us, before a bemused grin tugged at his thin lips.

"Why, look who we have here. Getting reacquainted?"

Theresa flashed me a hot, seductive glance before gliding across the room to Valentine. "I'm finished with him now if you want a turn."

Valentine's lips curled up in disgust, but then he laughed. "Yes, well, I hope you kept your appetite, because master has something absolutely wicked prepared for dinner." His eyes locked with Theresa's for a moment, and had I not been watching, I wouldn't have noticed the way her back stiffened. Then Valentine's gaze moved to me and smug satisfaction settled onto his face. "I do hope you brought the lovely Piper. I have been most morose without her."

"Master is giving her a tour of the house as we speak." Theresa patted Valentine on the chest before pushing her way through the door, not giving me a passing glance.

Valentine, misreading my expression, sighed and then chuckled as he shook his head. "Ah, women, such mercurial creatures. They love you until they get what they want, then you're yesterday's blood bag." Valentine gestured to me with one hand and grinned. "Don't look so glum. There will be plenty of other pretty little things waiting to get a taste of your immortal cock. The night's young after all."

I kept my face neutral, not giving anything away. Not what Theresa said or how much I wanted to rip his throat out right that second. There would be time for that later, after we figured out how we were going to get out of here in one piece.

Chapter 3
Rayne

"THIS IS BULLSHIT," I growled, throwing my bag across my bedroom. It smacked the wall with a satisfying thud, crumbling the stone slightly under the impact. I would have been afraid of reprimand from our master, but I was too upset to think about any of that.

"Dude, take a chill pill." Drake collapsed on the dark brown suede couch sitting on one side of my room.

I say my room, but it wasn't really. It was the room I lived in for several decades before we moved to our own house hundreds of miles away from here. I wanted nothing more than to be back there now. To have my familiar things surrounding me, our basement getaway, and Piper's scent everywhere. But no, I was stuck in this cold stone tomb our master insisted on surrounding himself with.

Our rooms weren't even our own. We couldn't have things out that we liked, and we always had to be ready to play the host to him and his many warped friends. Which was often.

I pushed those dark thoughts away. Never again.

My hands gripped the posts of the ancient bed frame, my fingers biting into the wood with a crack. "First, Antoine, and now that asshole. He can't have her! He can't. Piper is *mine*," I snarled, and prepared to rip the posts from the bed, but Allister's hand came down on my arm, stopping me.

"Calm down. Do you want him to hear you? The walls have ears." Allister tapped his ear and circled his finger around the room. "We are all upset, but there's no need to get yourself killed over it."

"Yes, there is," I snapped back, jerking my arm from his grip and shoving him away. Or as far back as I could get him. The guy was built like a brick building.

Aw, our little brother's in love.

"Shut up," I barked at Drake, my head whipping in his direction. "Don't act like you don't care about her too."

Drake lifted a shoulder and dropped it. "I didn't say that, but then again you're the one poking around in my head." He tapped the side of his forehead with a grin.

I frowned. Some days, I hated that I could hear others' thoughts, everyone from the mailman to the people who were most important in my life. I could hear every single thought or inkling they had, whether I liked it or not. It did come in handy sometimes, but other times it made it hard to know if what was in my head was my thoughts or someone else's.

Look at that ass. That perky fine ass...ripe for the plucking. Oh, what I would do to shove my thick cock—

I grabbed my head with my hands and shoved the thoughts away. He's not here anymore. I don't have to do that anymore. I'm safe. I'm fine. He's gone now. Antoine saw to that.

"Rayne."

My eyes moved away from the place on the floor I'd been glaring a hole into and over to Wynn, who stepped into my room from the now open bedroom door. That lazy smirk was nowhere to be found on his too pretty face as he watched me. "Are you alright?"

I nodded but didn't answer.

Instead of asking out loud, Wynn pushed his thoughts at me. *He's gone, Rayne. He can't hurt you anymore.*

"I know," I snapped, jerking my eyes away from him, earning me a curious look from the twins.

"What's up?" Drake asked, leaning forward onto his knees. His eyes searched between Wynn and me.

"Nothing," I answered, before Wynn could out me. "He's just being an ass as usual."

Drake snorted. "Well, maybe you should stay out of our heads? There's a reason thoughts are supposed to be private."

I blew out a hard breath and rubbed a hand over my face with a dark laugh. "Fuck that. You think things to rile me up on purpose."

Drake chuckled. "You do have a point about that. However, you must admit, you've never been this worked up over a human before. And you haven't even banged her yet."

I grabbed the pillow off my bed and chucked it at him. "That's none of your business."

"Oh, ho, ho," Drake laughed, catching the pillow and throwing it back. I dodged it just in time. "It is very much my business, because I want her too."

A possessive part of me flared up, but I held back the urge to bare my fangs at him. I knew my brothers wanted Piper and that she felt things for them as well. It didn't mean I had to like it though. I was the one she doted on. I was the one she had almost...I groaned in frustration and collapsed on the edge of my bed, my head hanging between my arms and legs. "This sucks."

Allister snorted and clapped me on the back. "Welcome to love, little brother. It only gets worse from here."

I grunted, but didn't answer.

"How'd you get away from Theresa?" Drake turned from torturing me to Wynn. I was thankful for the reprieve. "I would think you'd be cock deep in her ass by now."

I didn't need to look up to see the pained expression on Wynn's face, since it was all in his head. The moment our master was out of sight, Theresa had plastered herself against Wynn, and tried all but stripping right there in the foyer to get him to come play with her. The woman had no tact or self-respect. Not like Piper. No, she was kind and well, I'd admit, a bit of a klutz, but she also had a fire in her that drew me like a moth to her flame and I didn't give a shit if she burned me to ash. I'd die with a smile on my face.

"You're thinking nauseatingly romantic things again, aren't you?" Drake grimaced, interrupting Wynn from his rehashing of his great escape. The other two looked to me as well.

I shifted in place, scowling. "No."

Allister laughed. "Yes you are. Don't deny it. I can see it plain as the nose on your face."

"Stop it," I growled and gestured to the door. "Don't you have your own room to hang out in? Why must you be in mine?"

To my surprise, Drake stood. "You're right. I do." He moved toward the door and bumped Wynn on his way. "I'm going to go rub one out. Who knew making Piper a servant would make her even more

41

tantalizing?" He licked his lips lasciviously and winked. "Maybe I'll get a chance to taste her next?"

I jumped to my feet, intent on beating his face in, but he was gone, laughing down the hallway before I got the chance. Allister moved around me toward the door. "You leaving too?"

Allister sighed and shook his head. "I better go make sure he actually goes to his room. We don't need any hiccups on this trip. We'll be lucky if we all get out a live at this rate."

"Too true." Wynn inclined his head, moving from his place by the door and folding into the spot Drake had left. "You don't mind if I hide out here for a while, do you?" He didn't really seem to be asking, since he had already stretched out on my couch, his arm tossed over his eyes.

I shut the door behind Allister and went to get my discarded luggage. "You don't think being in my room will keep Theresa away, do you?"

Without moving his arm away from his face, Wynn sighed and answered, "No, but it will take her longer to find me. Plus, she's never had any love for you."

I shook my head and scoffed, "You mean, she doesn't like me picking through her demented head. I know what goes on in that thing and it's enough to give me nightmares." I shuddered, propping my suitcase on my bed. I unzipped it and began the tedious process of removing my clothing from the bag and placing them in the dresser. Usually, Piper or Darren would do this job, but seeing as Piper was otherwise detained—regrettably—and Darren...well, he had disappeared into Antoine's room and I hadn't seen him since.

Wynn hummed and lifted his arm briefly. "What are we going to do about Piper?"

I turned to him sharply. "What do you mean?"

Sitting up from the couch, Wynn's blue eyes locked on to me with more than a curious expression. "Well, you love her..."

Brows furrowed, I cocked my head to the side. "Yes?"

"Is that a question? Don't you know?" *Perhaps we were wrong. Maybe he only wants a place to wet his—*

"Fuck you." I stomped across the room and shoved a finger at him. "You don't get to judge me. You, the one who is basically

43

more incubus than vampire. And for your information, yes, I do love Piper. Not that I've told her as much yet but there, does that satisfy your inquisition?"

Wynn arched a brow but didn't get angry, he rarely did. "I was simply curious to know how far you would go for her. Would you go against Antoine for her?"

"Yes," I snapped without hesitation.

Amusement twinkled in Wynn's eyes. "Would you defy our master for her?"

"In a heartbeat."

Leaning forward so his face was close to mine, Wynn's voice lowered. "Would you die for her?"

With my jaw set, I made sure my voice carried the weight of my words. "A thousand times over."

Wynn stared at me for a long time and I tried to read his mind, but it was either blank or he was putting up a wall. After what felt like forever, Wynn smiled that infuriatingly smug grin of his and leaned back. "Good, because you might actually have to."

Chapter 4

Antoine

BEHIND THE SAFETY OF my bedroom walls, I jerked at my tie with more force than necessary.

Things were spiraling out of my control. I was the head of my household, I should have a better grip on things than I did. Worse yet, the moment my master stepped in, I was back to being at his beck and call. It was like I hadn't made a stand all those years ago.

I let my tie hang loose and worked on my cuffs as I stared hard at the bed. My bedroom was the same as it had been fifty years ago. Same comforter and sheets in a dark crimson color—one I had made sure never graced my bedroom back at Durand manor. The mahogany bedposts taunted me with all the dark and awful memories from this room. One would think that being my master's favorite would save me from his depravity, but it only seemed to make him more set on molding me to be like him.

Back then, I'd done a fine job pretending he was changing me. Warping me the way he had warped Valentine. Though, I had a feeling Valentine was already fucked up before he was turned.

I didn't want to be back in this room. I certainly didn't want Piper in here with me. I let out a dark chuckle, thinking of how she was going to react when she realized she had to share my room with Darren *and me.* Darren was used to it. We bonded because we wanted to, not because I was forced to. I certainly didn't think Piper would take sharing my room in stride the same way Darren did.

My human servant in question moved around my room, putting up our things without a word. His emotions were harder to read today, but I had a feeling he was holding back his feelings more for my

46

benefit than anything. Piper sure as hell wasn't.

From the moment I bound her to me, I knew she was going to be different. She felt everything so much...*more.* Every emotion was heightened to the billionth degree. Her confusion and hurt at my not being there when she woke, to the anger at my blatant dismissal of her, was broadcasted loudly. I didn't want to hurt her. It wasn't my intention, but I had to build a wall between us if either of us were going to survive this visit. My brothers already showed their feelings for her too easily. Boris had no doubt picked up on it the same way he had picked up on my mark on her. After thousands of years, I would think that he would have lost some of his strength, but if anything, time had done nothing but make him stronger and his outsides more grotesque.

Hands touched my shoulders and I allowed Darren to help me shrug out of my jacket. I worked on the buttons of my white shirt while Darren hung my jacket up to be cleaned later. My eyes followed him around the room, waiting for him to say something. I knew he wanted to. He might keep his opinion to himself in front of others, but behind closed doors he didn't usually wait too long to let me have it.

"You need to talk to her." Ah, there it was.

"Why?" was the only response I gave him. I knew my reasons, but I wasn't going to tell him. He might seem like the obedient servant, but Darren defied me more than anyone knew. He was just good at hiding it.

Darren paused in his smoothing of the jacket's sleeve, his gloved hands hovering in midair. He had taken to wearing them after we were bonded. Darren had told me the change had made everything feel different, more, just more. It was hard for him to cope with the new sensations and so I bought him a pair of gloves to deal with it. I thought eventually he would stop wearing them, but it seemed to have turned into more of a habit than anything else.

"I'm sure I do not need to tell you that Piper is confused and hurt by your behavior toward her." Darren slowly turned around to face me. His face a mask of indifference although his words were laced with disapproval. "I remember how it was when I changed. I couldn't imagine what it would have been like if you had treated me the way you are treating her."

My lips ticked up at the sides. Oh, I remembered as well. Almost the moment after he woke up, we found ourselves with an appetite for each other we couldn't quite slake. I felt it for Piper as well, my cock hadn't softened since the moment I'd been inside her, both fangs and cock. Remembering how she felt, how she tasted, and how she sounded as I took from her and then poured myself into her was torture. All I wanted right now was to find her and drag her back to this room to take her again and again, until I could get her out of my damn mind and veins.

No matter how much I wanted to, I couldn't. She wasn't mine. Piper had my mark and to everyone who wasn't us, she technically belonged to me. But she didn't, not really. She was ours. My brothers and mine. If anyone had claim to her, it wouldn't be me.

"I am doing what is best for us all," I finally replied to Darren, before taking a seat on the bed to remove my shoes. Darren beat me to it, kneeling before me to unlace my dress shoes. My cock twitched in my slacks at the sight.

"Best for her? Or best for you?" Darren didn't look up from my shoes as he removed one and then the other. My socks were next, but he didn't move from the floor. His hands moved up my legs until they rested on my thighs. Those dark eyes met mine with an intensity I hadn't seen in a long time.

My mouth watered at the same time that my brows furrowed. "You care for her?"

Darren's face softened. "I would be remiss if I didn't."

He shifted to leave, but I grabbed his hand, keeping him before me. I held him by the wrist and pulled his glove off one finger at a time, loving every gasp he let out as I released him from the white cloth. "Do not try to hide from me, Darren." Tugging him closer by his hand, until he was a hairsbreadth away, I searched his face. "I see you." My mouth captured his, causing him to grunt but not in protest. He pushed back just as fervently, his teeth nipping at my lips. The first time we'd kissed like this he'd bit me, and I had ended up rolling on the floor laughing, unable to continue. For a human to be the one to bite during a simple kiss had been too much for me. Even now it made my lips twitch.

"Stop it," Darren grumbled against my lips, his hands going to my shoulders before pushing me back. I fell onto the bed, and the mattress sunk, air puffing up around me from the lack of use. Darren straddled my lap, his hands going to where my shirt, previously unbuttoned, fell open. Using his teeth to remove his other glove, he settled his hands on my stomach. My abs twitched beneath them. "You forget, I see you as well."

I groaned as Darren rolled his hips, our cocks rubbing against one another. I was too close to the edge already, and without much more stimulation and I would burst.

Placing one hand in the middle of my chest, Darren leaned forward until our noses brushed. "You are scared."

"N—" I tried to argue, but Darren pressed his finger to my mouth.

"I'm talking."

I resisted the urge to roll my eyes at him. Darren was not a top. He'd never be one, but when he wanted something, he definitely knew how to play the part. So, I waited for him to get to the point so I could sink my cock into him.

"Piper makes you feel things you've never allowed yourself to feel before." He paused for a moment, a pensive look crossing his face before he continued, "Even for me." I stared up at him, looking for some kind of hurt in his expression, but there was none, even the feelings he was projecting were content. The way he was acting made me think he was going to act like a jealous lover, but it seemed I didn't quite know my servant as well as I thought.

He ground his hips against me again. "You want her." I grunted but didn't deny it, setting my hands on his hips and encouraging him to keep going. "More than you want to admit to yourself. But from the moment she walked into our house, you couldn't keep your eyes off her. Even now. This," he reached between us to cup my hard cock in his hand, "isn't for me, it's for her. The bonding might have been made to protect her, but you wanted her and felt for her long before you sank anything into her soft flesh." There was something in the way he said it that made me pause and really look at him.

I opened my mouth to comment on what I saw, but Darren had pulled me from my slacks and jerked his hand up my length. My eyes closed briefly, and my hip thrust up into his hand. I was strung too tight. Hard for too long. I exploded into his hand after only a few strokes.

Darren moved to get off me, but I grabbed him by the lapels of his perfectly ironed suit and pushed him down onto the bed. With a fang-toothed grin, I growled, "My turn."

Chapter 5

Piper

I WAS SWEATING BUCKETS and I was sure that Count Boris Whatchamajig could smell it with every step I took. The master vampire had moved his arm from around my shoulders, thankfully to escorting me by the arm like a real gentleman. Not that I would ever use that word in the same sentence as Boris. He might act the quirky foreigner, but from my masters' caution of him and his rapid punishment of Theresa, I wasn't fooled. He was a monster. A killer. Everything I had expected my masters to be and more.

He'd made Valentine after all.

Then again, in that line of thought, Boris had made all of my masters. Does that mean they were evil in some way as well? Or are they good despite their upbringing? Ugh. My head hurt.

"And this would be the drawing room." Boris waved an arm at a room with chairs and no art equipment whatsoever.

"Where's the drawing stuff?" I inquired, before I could stop myself and then stiffened as Boris quieted.

"You know...I never quite thought of that. I suppose it wasn't always called a drawing room. Once, it was called a withdrawing room, some place to go with your guests to have privacy. Even to meet with the king, but that was then." He leaned in close to me as if we were the best of friends sharing a secret. "We must come up with a new name for this room before you leave. Yes?" I nodded quickly. "Good. Now, where else can I show you? Ah." He turned toward a set of double doors. "Here is the library. Do you like to read?"

I opened my mouth to answer, but Marcus grunted behind me. I shot a glance to him, but whatever message he was trying to convey with his Neanderthal grunts was lost on me. I turned back to the count and said, "I admit I don't read as much as I should. Mostly, I read lighter things, like—"

"Romance?" Boris finished for me with a twinkle in those blood-red eyes. The amusement on his face made me almost forget who he was and where I was, but then one look at those long fangs and I remembered.

Swallowing thickly, I nodded. "Yeah. Yes. Romances. I was never the best student."

Boris laughed and patted my hand. "Never fear dear, your secret is safe with me, and of course Marcus. Isn't that right, boy?" He glanced over his shoulder at Marcus who was three of Boris put together. The very fact that Boris called Marcus—the behemoth of a man—a boy, wasn't lost on me. It was hilarious in an ironic, dark sort of way. One that I didn't want to think about much right now.

Marcus didn't grunt in response as I expected, but in a low, gravelly voice that did weird things to my insides, replied, "Yes, master."

"See?" Boris turned back to me with a grin. "Perfectly safe." His lips dipped down for a moment as Marcus pulled open the library door for us. "However, I do not think the kinds of romance I have would suit your needs. Most of my collection are from my travels and many aren't even in English. You know, I have one of the original copies of *A Midsummer Night's Dream* written by the Shakespeare himself."

My mouth dropped open in surprise and I couldn't help the excitement that filled me. "Really? Did you meet him?"

"Oh yes." Boris inclined his head with a joyful look on his face. "William was quite the poet, but also a drunkard. He never could get his words out right because of all the drink he'd indulged in the night before. If not for his friend Francis, he would never have gotten anything out at all."

Astonished by the story, I wondered at the ability to have actually been places and met people who no one could say they knew. I could just imagine going back in time and meeting my favorite singers and writers in the prime of their life. To have lived for so long and to have met so many people...I envied him and his long life. Then, I remembered mine was long now as well. A hundred years from now, if Antoine still lived, then I would still be exactly as I am now. I could see history change right before my eyes.

"You don't sound Russian." The words tumbled out of my mouth before I could think better of them.

Amusement filled Boris's eyes before he led us into the library. "I'm glad you say so. I have worked hard to perfect the modern American accent. It makes blending in with the local populous so much easier."

I stared at him for a moment, wondering how to ask the next question. But there was no need. The look on my face apparently said everything and Boris laughed once more.

"Do not look so skeptical, Piper. People believe what they want to believe." I didn't like the way the master vampire said my name. It felt like worms twisting inside of me, trying to get out.

"And what do they believe?" I glanced back at Marcus. He walked closely behind us, but not close enough to help if Boris suddenly turned feral.

"Here, let us rest." Boris brought us to a sitting area in the middle of the library and offered me a seat. I happily released his arm and sat down, only to wish I was standing once more when he sat beside me, his thigh pressing against mine. Marcus didn't sit. Nor did Boris ask him to. He stood there like a handsome statue waiting for his next command.

"In this modern age, it isn't unlikely for someone such as myself to wander down the streets." Boris gave me a full-fanged smile. "Society has learned to not question the weird or unusual lest you offend someone. They're more worried about getting sued for questioning me than for their own safety." He laughed in such a way that my feet shifted beneath me, urging me to run. "They'd call my unique features a fad. Or maybe even a deformity. Some might even say I was trendy." He used air quotes, as if it were the most normal thing for a thousand-year-old vampire to do.

I hummed and put up a brave face. "I could see that. Books and television have really desensitized the masses."

Boris scoffed and rolled his eyes. "Ugh. Television. Movies. Vampires that sparkle. Or explode into a bucket of blood. Can you imagine? What will they think of next?"

Either I was brain-dead or had a total disregard for my own survival, but the next question was out of my mouth before

I could decide which. "What does happen?"

Boris gave me a sideways look.

Clearing my throat, I looked at Marcus and then back to Boris. "When you die. I mean."

Boris leaned forward, a smile spreading across his lips. "Why, my dear, are you planning on killing one of us?"

I gave a nervous laugh and shook my head. "Well, you know...if I ever wanted to die myself."

There was a long silence that made my heart race and my eyes dart to Marcus once more for help. The large man made no move to help. His nostrils flared and his jaw tightened, which was the only clear evidence that he was even paying attention.

"I do hope," Boris began again softly, his rough hands taking mine once more, "that if it ever comes to that, you will turn to me for aid and not take out one of my beloved boys. I would so much hate to lose them."

Licking my lips, I nodded. "Of course."

"Now." Boris stood, bringing me along with him whether I wanted to or not. "I think that's enough of a tour for one day. You'll have plenty of time to see the rest of the house over the course of the week. And if you ever get lost, please don't hesitate to call out." He tapped his long, pointed ear with a twinkle in those blood-red eyes. "Someone will hear you."

Resigned to never call out for help in this house, I followed Boris out of the library and down the hall, back the way we came, before he led me up the stairs and down a long corridor not unlike the one back at the House of Durand. Several doors lined the walls, each composed of a dark wood I couldn't identify. The floors were hardwood with a reddish-brown tint. A color I hoped was manufactured and not from a sloppy eater.

"You'll find that we have renovated the house to keep up with the times," Boris explained, gesturing around the hallway at the pane windows and light sockets, before leaning in to fake whisper, "No one wants to do their business in an outhouse, believe me. Some things even I wish I wasn't alive for."

I laughed politely. Really, I was counting down the seconds until he would release me to my room. I wanted to scrub every inch of my body until I didn't feel his creepy hands on it anymore.

"And here is your room." Boris stopped before the third door and turned to me. Lifting my hand to his mouth, he hovered above, it inhaling my scent, before laying his mouth on the top of it. I held back my cringe as he straightened. "It was a pleasure to get to know you and I hope we have another chance for a one-on-one chat again soon. After all, we have forever."

I gave him a blinding smile, even as my stomach plummeted.

"Marcus." Boris inclined his head to the large vampire, before sauntering down the hallway to god knew where. I didn't give a shit as long as he was away from me.

When the master vampire was good and gone, I turned to Marcus and opened my mouth, but he pressed his finger to his lips, giving me a stern look. I clapped my mouth shut and turned back to my room. He was right. It wasn't safe to talk here. I wasn't even sure it would be safe to talk in the confines of my own bedroom. A bedroom that was already occupied.

I frowned at the door, listening for the voices I'd heard just a second ago. There it was again. Two sets. My brows furrowed

62

as I turned to doorknob and pushed the door open.

The sight before me made my face heat. I averted my eyes. "W-What are you doing in my room?" I stuttered out, trying to look anywhere but at the two half naked men in my bed. It was obvious what Antoine and Darren had been doing with the former kneeling before the latter. Something I would definitely be putting away for later, but still, it was a bit disconcerting.

"Actually..." Antoine stood and approached me. My eyes darted to his bare chest beneath his unbuttoned shirt, trailing along the firm muscle and the house sigil tattooed over his heart just like the others. My gaze slid down his abs—yum—to the pale hair disappearing into his unbuttoned pants. Antoine made a sound in the back of his throat, a mix between a growl and a pained sound, before clearing his throat. "This is my room."

My eyes snapped back to his face. Any arousal I was feeling was shoved aside as confusion took its place. "Your room? Why would I be taken to..."

Antoine arched a perfectly pale brow at me.

My mouth dropped open as I let my eyes wander around the room to where my bag, and Darren's, sat next to Antoine's already unpacked one. The bed, a larger than king-sized bed, sat in the middle of the room, the sheets already rumpled. Darren busied himself by fixing it while I confronted Antoine.

Turning back to him, I closed my mouth with a snap before narrowing my eyes on my employer. "I'm not staying in here."

"Yes, you are."

"No, I'm not." I twisted on my heel and marched toward the door, but Antoine grabbed my wrist and pulled me back. "Let go. I'm going to go talk to Boris. He must have been mistaken. I can't stay here with you." I shook my head over and over as Marcus and Darren looked on with neutral expressions.

"You can and you will," Antoine commanded me, the feel of his power brushed over my skin, but not like before when I learned of their true origins and he'd convinced me to stay. Convinced, as in used this vampire superpowers to 'persuade' me to do as he wished.

I crossed my arms over my chest and smirked at him. "Funny, I don't think I will." I cocked my head to the side and stared hard into those pale blue eyes. This asshole fucked me, bit me, and then left me alone to figure things out by myself. I wasn't about to make things easy for him now.

Antoine let out an exasperated growl and dragged a hand over his face. "Piper, you do not understand the predicament we are in. This isn't a game. You can't defy me just because you cannot have your way. We're in my master's house. *Boris,* as you call him, does not take defiance lightly."

"I'm not defying him. I'm simply demanding the same as any other human. Privacy. A place I can call my own. Now, is that so much to ask for?" I gave him a sickly-sweet smile, but if anything, it only made his face harden further.

"Yes." Antoine reached out and brushed my hair away from my neck, his fingers trailing over the scar there, and I shivered. "You bear my mark, which in the eyes of every vampire means you are *mine.*" His eyes flashed with something dark and possessive before his lips tipped up at the edges as those pale orbs met mine. "That is what you wanted, right?"

I swallowed and nodded.

Antoine leaned in so our noses were inches apart. "Well, as they say...you should have read the fine print." Pulling away from me, Antoine moved back to his discarded shoes and sat down on the bed. Darren, without being asked, proceeded to help him put them on. "As you can see, being a human servant doesn't just come with perks. They come with conditions. Conditions that you will now have to abide by if you want to stay in my household and not join Valentine's," his jaw clenched as he said the vampire's name, "ranks."

Clearing my throat, I jerked my head toward the bed. "And part of those conditions is that we have to share a room?"

Antoine chuckled as he buttoned the cuffs of his shirt. "This is *my* room. You are merely here to serve me. In any way I require." His eyes were hot as they swept up and down my form.

I tightened my arms around myself, both liking and hating the way he looked at me right now. Knowing he could feel what I felt, I pushed my apprehension down and pulled on as much rage as I could manage. My days of being my own person were gone. Now, I would have to erect even more walls around myself. Ones that couldn't be torn down. Even by me.

Chapter 6
Drake

An hour and a good wank later, Wynn knocked on my bedroom door. I opened it, not bothering to button my pants completely or put on a shirt. He didn't care one way or the other in any case.

"Where's your brother?" Wynn asked, his tone all business-like, completely unlike him. His eyes kept skittering around the hallway, not quite meeting mine.

My brows bunched and I frowned. "In his room, I'd imagine. What's going on?"

Wynn shook his head, telling me to be quiet. "Not here. Get your brother and meet me in Antoine's room. We don't have long. Hurry." With that, he turned on his heel and walked over to Antoine's door, not bothering to knock before he entered. I could hear Piper's voice in there already, as well as Rayne's. With the least worrisome of us with his panties in a wad, I hurried to my brother's room. I rapped on the door once before opening it. Allister had his back to me as he stood in front of the mirror, buttoning up his shirt.

"Did you forget what we look like already?" I joked, clapping him on the shoulder with a laugh. "You'd think after all these years you'd be sick of looking at your ugly mug."

Allister shook his head and pushed me away with a roll of his eyes. "It's your ugly mug too, you know."

I struck a pose behind him in the mirror. "Nope, I'm the pretty one. You're the ugly duckling."

"Isn't that a nursery rhyme?" Allister asked over his shoulder, as he moved away from the mirror and over to where his shoes sat. "And we are identical twins. There's no logic to your assessment."

I shrugged. "Facts are facts, brother. Anyway, we're needed in Antoine's room. Chop-chop." I clapped my hands together and walked to the door.

"Aren't you forgetting something?" Allister inquired, nodding at my bare chest.

I smirked. "Nope."

"This wouldn't have to do with a certain blonde maid, would it?" Allister sighed as we walked down the hallway and toward Antoine's room.

Grinning from ear to ear, I shrugged. "What can I say? I need all the advantages I can get. Antoine's already bound to her. Rayne's one apology away from getting into her panties. And we don't have to even guess about Wynn. He'll have her spread-eagle in his bed before this week is through. I have to up my game if I want to compete with that."

Laughing at me, Allister knocked on Antoine's door but I opened it before anyone could answer. They were waiting for us inside regardless, there was no need to be polite.

Antoine's room looked the same way it had when we lived here before. The same as mine and Allister's. It was like we'd never left. Even the screams and the stink of blood still haunted the rooms. I didn't know how I was ever going to get any sleep tonight.

I passed Marcus, who was standing by the door, and stepped into the room. My eyes drifted from Wynn and Rayne sitting on Antoine's couch, to Antoine leaning against his wardrobe with Darren close at his side, to Piper sitting on the edge of the bed. She looked pissed as she worried her bottom lip between her teeth. She kept shooting glowers at Antoine—who was firmly ignoring her—but when my brother and I walked into the room, her eyes shot to us. Those pale brown orbs scanned over Allister briefly before landing me. Her eyes widened and the tiny pink muscle in her mouth darted out to wet her lips. The air in the room filled with the sweet, sweet scent of her arousal, making the others shift uncomfortably.

"See," I muttered to my brother, who rolled his eyes before collapsing on the couch next to Rayne.

I knew exactly what I looked like. While I hadn't planned on seeing her after I'd just gotten out of the shower, it was a side benefit. My hair was still slightly wet and curled around my ears, and my skin gleamed from the moisture. I looked good, and by Piper's state of arousal, she thought I did too.

I smirked at Piper, causing her to gasp and turn her eyes back to Wynn who had called us here.

"Theresa had some interesting things to tell me today." Wynn sat as stiffly as a corpse on the other end of the couch, his face still set in a serious frown.

I took up residence against the post of the bed, near enough to smell Piper's sweet scent but far enough away to tempt her into giving me sideways looks. Responding to Wynn's words, I muttered with a smirk, "Oh, I bet she did. I bet Theresa was all kinds of chatty while she was riding your magic rod."

Piper frowned and a flash of hurt crossed her face. I wished I could take back my words, but it was too late. Fuck me.

Wynn ignored my poke—another abnormality—as his eyes locked onto Antoine. "She says this is a trap. We're all in great danger."

Allister snorted. "Like we didn't know this already?" My brother looked around the room. "Who here didn't think this was a trap before we even got on the plane?" He raised his hand and waited for someone else to agree. No one did. "See?" He dropped his hand. "This is old news, Wynn."

"What exactly did Theresa say?" Antoinc askcd, not lctting my brother deter Wynn's worry. "Did she have any other information that could help us? Or just that we're all in danger?"

I scoffed and shook my head. "I doubt she could get it out with his dick in her mouth."

Piper froze next to me, and once again I wanted to take back my words. I had to stop doing that. I was so used to screwing with Wynn about his womanizing ways— the guy fed on sex, for crying out loud— that it was hard not to poke at him now. Though, judging by the way Piper was reacting, I wasn't winning any points for pointing it out.

This time Wynn didn't ignore me. He jumped to his feet and was across the room in an instant, his fist flying for my face. I ducked just in time and the wood above my head shattered as Wynn's fist went through it. Darting to the side, I held my hands up in peace. "I was just messing with you, bro. Why are you so worked up?"

Wynn gnashed his fangs at me. "All of our lives are at stake—Piper's in particular—and you make jokes about how I got the information? You should be kissing my feet for taking one for the team. We could all be dead in our beds tomorrow."

"And what a burden that would have been," I quipped, unable to help myself. I dodged Wynn's fist again before Marcus stepped between us.

"Enough."

"Marcus is right," Antoine announced, stroking his fingers across his chin. "This is not the time to be fighting amongst ourselves. We have much greater threats to deal with. Now, if you can keep your mouth shut long enough for Wynn to tell us what he knows, maybe we'll all get out of this place alive. If not in one piece."

Wynn and I stared at each other for a long, hard minute before I conceded with a nod. "Fine. I'll knock off the jokes."

"Thank you." Antoine turned to Wynn and gestured with a hand. "If you would continue?"

Wynn crossed his arms over his chest and stared at the ground. "Apparently, Valentine had a little more to say about us from his visit than just about Piper."

74

Piper's breathing increased and her pulse raced at the mention of Valentine. I didn't blame her. The guy was a freak. "Our master believes we have strayed too far from the ways he has taught us. That we are becoming too mainstream."

Rayne laughed bitterly, leaning forward on his knees as he propped his face on his hands. "That's a bit hypocritical. He's the one who made sure no one could tell he's from Russia, but didn't do shit about his face."

Scattered chuckles spread across the room. I stepped forward into the middle of the group. "So, that's it? He wants us to be more monster-like?"

Wynn blew out a hard breath. "I wish. Not only is he going to be looking to see if we have forgotten the old ways, but he is going to be testing our feelings toward..." He trailed off as his eyes moved over to Piper.

Piper shifted on the bed, her arms wrapping around herself. "Don't hold back on my account. I'm part of this too, you know. No going back now."

"She's right," Allister interjected, smiling at her. The cheeky bastard. "Piper's immortal now. If we keep things like this from her then we might as well sign her death certificate ourselves." He jerked his chin toward Wynn. "Tell her. Let's get it all out there so we can figure out how to leave here alive."

Wynn hesitated for a moment, shooting a look at Antoine. Our head of house nodded, though he didn't look happy about it. Tucking his hands into his pockets, Wynn shifted his stance toward Piper. "Valentine wants you. We all know he already called Antoine and tried to buy you. He's pissed that you're a human servant now, but don't think that's going to stop him. In fact, it might just make him even more adamant to have you."

Piper stood abruptly. "Wait, I thought this was supposed to keep me safe? Why'd I go through all that crap if Valentine can still get to me?"

Antoine shot her a look. "You went through that crap so that he couldn't snatch you out of your bed in the middle of the night without a word."

"Oh, gee, thanks. So what now, he has to what? Ask permission?" she snapped back, her hands on her hips and her eyes glowing with fire. God, she was beautiful and she didn't give two shits about who Antoine was. If God made a perfect woman, it was Piper Billings.

"More or less," Wynn answered for Antoine with a sigh. He closed the few between them and placed his hands on her shoulders. "We won't let him touch you. I promise. We are doing all of this to protect you. Valentine and our master can play their games, but you belong with us. Don't let it worry you."

Piper touched one of his hands tenderly and jealousy flared in me. I wanted to be that guy. I'd never been in a position where I wanted to be Wynn in my entire existence, except for this very moment. She peered up at him lovingly, with those big doe eyes, and smiled softly. "I know you will. But I'm going to worry regardless."

"Can you get on with the rest?" Rayne complained, his face tight with irritation. I wasn't the only one annoyed by Wynn getting all the attention. "We have a dinner to go to in a few minutes and I, for one, don't want our master to send someone to look for us."

"Rayne has a point," Allister noted and stood. "We should prepare for whatever they are going to through at us tonight."

"Why do you think they will start tonight?" I turned to my brother with a frown. "Wouldn't they be more subtle about it?"

My brother laughed. "You should know as well as I, that subtlety has never been our master's style. He'll want to get his intentions out as soon as possible."

"Meaning dinner tonight will be the first test." Antoine moved away from the wardrobe and dropped his arms to his sides, his eyes scanning all of us. "Every action you make will be studied. Every word you say will be scrutinized. We made it perfectly clear during Valentine's visit that Piper is ours, so there is no need to hold back our affection. But we must all be in agreement." His eyes settled on each of us, but stopped on Marcus and hardened. "We must show a combined force. They will be less likely to try to take Piper if we show them that they'd have to take us all out to have her."

I watched the silent exchange between Antoine and Marcus, while Antoine talked to the rest of the room. It was clear that out of the six vampires in the room, Marcus was the weak link in it all. He had made it clear that he didn't want Piper here and didn't agree to having her become a servant. If our master could get to anyone, it would be through him.

"And the rest of it?" I questioned, stepping closer to Piper and Wynn. "What about the tests? Should we act the way we normally would or pretend we have not conformed to the masses?"

Antoine stared off into the distance for a second, before closing his eyes briefly. When he opened them, his gaze had the same look in them they had all those years ago, holding a tortured but feral hunger that curled his lips into a cruel smile. "Let us give the master what he wants. And let the rest follow."

Chapter 7
Piper

"YOU HAVE GOT TO be kidding me." I gaped at the full-length gown Darren had laid out for me to wear to dinner. Gown was being generous. The thing barely had any material to it. The fabric it did have was pale blue tulle, which fell in strips down to the ground and up around the hanger, where I assumed my breasts would go. The only saving grace to the dress was a thicker piece of blue material beneath the skirt that would cover my private bits. The part that worried me most, however, was the strategically placed flower buds that covered the tulle. I figured they were there to cover up the important parts of my breasts, but that still left a whole lot of boob to be seen.

Darren sighed in exasperation. "We are trying to make a statement here. We need to—"

"I thought we were trying to make me less appealing?" I interrupted Darren with a scowl. "Not tempt Valentine like a dog with a bone."

Darren lifted his eyes to the heavens. "You have a great deal to learn about vampires."

I sighed and slipped my shoes off as I worked on disrobing. I didn't have to worry about the guys, since they'd all scattered to their own rooms to get ready, leaving me with Darren and Antoine. Antoine hid in the bathroom where he was preparing for tonight's festivities, letting Darren break the news of my clothes. Coward.

It should bother me to undress in front of Darren, but I didn't see how I was going to get into that thing by myself. I pulled my shirt over my head and groaned. "Is it weird that I miss the slutty maid outfit?"

Darren's lips ticked up at the edges. "It was quite entertaining."

81

When I got down to my bra and panties, I placed my hands on my hips and looked over the dress. I was not going to be able to wear my underwear or my bra with this. Fuck.

My eyes skipped over to Darren. His dark eyes were locked on to my form, confusing me. If I didn't know any better, I'd say he was checking me out.

"Darren." His dark eyes jerked up to mine when I said his name, and that neutral mask fell over his face, hiding what he was really thinking. With a slight smile, I turned to him and struck a what I hoped was seductive pose. "Are you checking me out?"

Not even bothered by my question, Darren adjusted his gloves before clearing his throat and putting his hands behind his back. "I have eyes and you are a very lovely woman."

I blushed. Pulling my lower lip into my mouth, I peered up at Darren beneath my eyelashes. "Why, Darren, you old charmer you. I didn't know you had eyes for anyone other than Antoine." I cocked my head to the side as I watched his reaction.

Darren's lips twitched. "My relationship with Master Durand is a complicated one, which has not kept me from enjoying the fairer sex."

"Fairer sex?" I grinned. "I never understood that phrase. Are we fairer because we are weaker? Or prettier?"

Darren let out an exasperated sigh. "And once again you ruin it by opening your mouth."

I stuck my tongue out at him playfully before giggling. "Still, it's nice to know I can draw even your eye."

Letting out a snort, Darren moved over to the bed where the dress was laid out. "You have five immortal vampires who are more than happy to show you how attractive you are. I certainly don't think you need to add another admirer to the mix."

I flushed. "Yeah. Well, they might want to screw me, but physical attraction can only get your so far..." I trailed off, my eyes going to the dress as my fingers played with the tulle skirt. "Especially when you have forever."

Darren was quiet for a moment, and then he placed a hand on my shoulder. My eyes drifted up to meet his gaze. "How are you? With the changes and everything?"

I sighed and looked at the dress once more. Lifting it up, I searched for a zipper or some way into the scrap of material. "It's strange, I guess. I don't know how to describe it. It's like...it's like..."

"Every nerve ending has been hyped up to a million?" Darren offered with a small smile. "It ties around the neck."

"Huh?" My mouth fell open as I stared at him in confusion. Then I realized he was talking about the dress. Giving him a sheepish grin, I turned the dress around and stepped into the solid piece of the skirt. I wiggled into it, not removing my underwear or bra just yet. No need to give Darren more of a show than he was getting. "Could you?" I turned and lifted my hair so he could tie the top around my neck.

The soft material of Darren's gloves brushed my neck where Antoine's scar sat, and I shivered. A hot flash of need raced through me and I swallowed it down. Pull it together for Christ's sake. This was Darren we're talking about. Anal. Clean freak. No fun. Darren.

"Don't worry," Darren murmured, as he finished tying the top. "The sensitivity will wane...a bit."

I gave a harsh laugh. "That's encouraging. Good to know that I won't be horny all the time." A voice cleared. My head jerked up and I locked eyes with the pale blue orbs of Antoine. My face heated to a million degrees as I realized what I'd just said in front of him.

"Antoine, uh, hey, Darren and I were just talking about, uh, you know, side effects." I shifted from foot to foot, feeling pretty ridiculous wearing this piece of nothing on top of my bra, while Antoine was dressed in a spanking new suit that made him look even more the dashing vampire lover than before. Plus, the unbuttoned shirt and loose tie around his neck was definitely doing things to my panties.

Antoine hummed as his eyes scanned over my form.

Before he could make a comment about it, I reached back and unsnapped my bra. "I was just finishing up when you..." I grunted, struggling to get the straps of my bra off and out from beneath the sheer fabric, and not flash Antoine my boobs. Darren saw me struggling and reached out to help, but I smacked his hands away. "I've got it." I scowled and turned my back on them to get it out from beneath, before readjusting my tits into the right position. Happy that all the parts that were supposed to be covered were covered, I turned back around. "There. All done."

Antoine's lips ticked up on one side before turning his attention to Darren. "Marcus was looking particularly unhappy with the plan. Have Wynn go speak with him."

I couldn't tell if he was asking or telling, but either way, Darren inclined his head and gave me one final look before heading out the door, leaving me alone with Antoine. Great.

"Uh, so..." I trailed off, clucking my tongue and snapping my fingers, trying to quell the nerves inside of me that came from being so near him. I didn't know how I was going to sleep tonight. "Darren said something about not knowing anything about vampires. That this," I gestured at the skimpy dress, "wouldn't be taunting Valentine into, you know, biting me."

Antoine strolled around the bed to where I stood, his eyes moving up and down my form. God, I wished the bond went the other way around so I could feel what he was feeling. I was sure he knew how rattled my nerves were. He stopped before me and reached a single, long fingered hand out to trace the line of the tulle at my neck, then down between my chest where the material split, before meeting the fabric at my waistline. Wherever his finger touched me burned, and I didn't know if I wanted him to stop or keep going.

"It's not a taunt," he finally answered, snapping me out of the trance I was in.

"What?"

"The dress. It's not a taunt." Antoine dropped his hand and met my eyes. "It's a declaration."

"Of what? 'Cause it sure feels like you guys just like to see what you can get me to dress up in." My eyes narrowed into slits. "Do you guys take bets? See who can get me to wear the most outrageous thing? 'Cause I'm telling you, if that's the case, someone's going to—"

"It's not." Antoine cut me off with a small smile that made my insides all gooey. "Think of it as a big fuck you to Valentine."

I snort laughed, my hand going up to my mouth to hide it. "Oh, is that right? So, you're pretty much doing the nana, nana, nana thing, huh?"

Antoine made a sound in the back of his throat. "Basically."

I hummed and laced my fingers in front of me, glancing down at the ground as awkwardness set in. This was the longest conversation we'd had since Antoine and I had sex. I was surprised he hadn't run away the moment he stepped out of the bathroom. But for once, Antoine wasn't leaving. He was standing there across from me looking as scrumptious and arrogant as ever, and I had nothing to say to him.

"You know," I began, finally finding my voice, clearing it as he met my gaze with those captivating icy blue orbs. "I should be mad at you. I still am," I added, as his lips twitched. "But in light of everything else going on, I guess I can put my anger on the back burner." Antoine started to say something, but I kept going. "For now."

Antoine watched me for a moment before taking a step closer to me. "I don't blame you, Piper, for being vexed with me." His eyes searched my face and trailed down my neck, lingering where he bit me. The nerves pulsed there as if craving his bite once more.

I resisted the urge to cover the bite mark with my hand.

"I am trying to do what's right," Antoine continued, his voice low as he seemed remarkably closer than before. My chest brushed against his jacket making my nipples pebble beneath the thin fabric.

"And leaving me to feel like a used piece of garbage was your go-to action?" I snapped, trying to cover my growing need with anger. "Because if that was your goal, you achieved it."

Antoine sighed and lowered his head slightly. "I cannot apologize more for my actions. I thought by pushing you away I was helping you. Helping the household. But..." He paused and lifted his head, his nose inches from mine. "Certain parties have made me aware of my bad judgment."

"You mean Darren ripped you a new one," I countered with a haughty glare that did nothing to cover up the quickening of my breath.

Those gorgeous lips twitched again. "Yes, well, I give as good as I get." Those words sounded far naughtier than they were probably supposed to, but it didn't keep my body from responding to them.

Antoine inhaled deeply and I flushed, knowing he could smell my reaction to him. Neither of us moved, our eyes locked in a never-ending stare off. I wasn't sure which one of us moved— and at the moment I didn't very well care—I just knew that Antoine's hands were on me and he tasted even better than when we first kissed. I chalked it up to my enhanced senses and wondered gleefully what else would be even more intense.

My thighs hit the mattress in a matter of seconds. A low stuttering gasp escaped from my throat as Antoine's mouth covered my nipple through the sheer fabric. Suddenly, I was thankful for the obscenity of the dress and hoped Antoine would rip it to shreds any second.

Shifting on top of me, Antoine settled between my thighs, pushing the strips of fabric away so that the tiny skirt rode up my legs, exposing my damp panties to the air. Long fingers found my folds beneath my panties and they thrust into me at the same pace as his tongue captured my mouth. My fingers curled into his hair, tugging him closer, and my legs wrapped around his waist, not able to get enough of him. Never being close enough. I grunted and gasped against his mouth with every move of his fingers and begged for more.

Tired of the foreplay, I reached down between us and grabbed the hardened length beneath his slack. Antoine released my mouth with a growl, his head arching back as he thrust into my hand. When I finally released him from his pants, and he was hot and heavy in my grasp, Antoine barred his fangs at me.

A small surprised cry came from my mouth, but he didn't try to bite me. Instead, he reached between us and guided himself to my opening. Our eyes locked as he slid home. Holding one of my legs up higher on his waist, he went deeper and harder than before. My eyes closed on their own as I gasped and writhed. I found myself going higher and higher as every nerve ending shot off in a sporadic symphony. When I was close to the edge, Antoine angled my head to the side. My eyes snapped open and there was a question in Antoine's gaze. One that only took me a fraction of a second to answer before I was tilting my head further for him.

This time, when Antoine's fangs pierced my skin, there was hardly any pain. There was a sharpness that only made the feel of him inside me even more sweet and I arched into it, wanting it harder, deeper. Antoine growled against my neck, his throat constricting under my hand where my fingers tangled on his nape. Each suck of my blood matched the movement of his hips, and that cliff I'd been dangling on dropped me like a sack of potatoes. My orgasm hit me hard and someone was screaming. It wasn't until I finally remembered how to breathe again that I realized the person screaming was me.

Chapter 8
Piper

THE DINING ROOM WAS much like the one back at the house. The table filling the middle of the room was longer than ours and held more people, but it was not any less creepy. There were no utensils or plates on the table, which made me more nervous than I already was.

Marcus sat to the right of Boris with one empty seat between them. Wynn was next to Marcus, looking lazily about the room. Rayne pouted where he sat by Wynn, with Allister taking up the furthermost seat at the end. On the other side, next to Allister, sat his brother and then Theresa, followed by Valentine with one empty seat between him and Boris.

Everyone knew. If it wasn't written all over my face, then the scent of what Antoine and I just did was still on both of us. It was clear from the way the occupants of the dining room stiffened and sniffed the air. There was a mixture of feelings that came along with it. Amusement, arousal, and anger. And that was just from my masters.

Theresa didn't seem bothered one way or the other, and was too busy giving Wynn moon eyes to care about me. Boris, who sat at the head of the table but who had stood for my arrival, had a delighted smirk on his lips. I wasn't sure what that was about, but I didn't care for it either. Anything that made that monster happy was something I wanted nothing to do with.

Then there was Valentine.

It was stupid of me to think he wouldn't show up. That perhaps he would be off gallivanting and terrorizing someone else while I was here. But there he was, sitting to the right of Boris with one seat between them. A look around the table gave me a bad feeling about that spot. The only other one was on the left side of Boris, and I had a nagging notion that it wasn't for me.

Surprisingly, the only person not at the table was Darren.

As if reading my mind, Antoine murmured, "Darren will be dining with the staff tonight."

My mouth puckered into an 'O' shape and I stopped walking, forcing Antoine to halt as well or drag me. "Well, then, I should join him. I wouldn't want him to get lonely."

"Nonsense," Boris called out with a wave of his hand. "A lovely creature such as yourself should never dine with the rabble. Besides, you got all dressed up and I wouldn't want you to waste such a lovely dress. Our Antoine seems to have already enjoyed it. It wouldn't be fair to rob the rest of us the chance to gaze upon your beauty."

I'd have blushed had the words not come from a grotesque monstrous being, whose only interest in me was torturing his underlings. Forcing a demure expression on my face, I gave a slight nod of my head. "Thank you for your compliments."

"Well," Boris chuckled, a sound that made my skin crawl, "they aren't free." My head jerked up at the words. "Please, come sit with me." He gestured to the chair between him and Valentine. Bile rose in my throat as Antoine squeezed my arm in warning.

With a tight nod, I let Antoine guide me around the dining table and to the seat Valentine had hurried to pull back for me. I tried to ignore him, but he was insistent, taking my hand in his as he pressed his lips to my knuckles.

"You are as beautiful as I remembered, Miss Billings," Valentine purred, stroking my hand with his fingers as I took my seat.

Antoine took my hand from Valentine's grasp with a vicious flash of fangs. "Durand. Piper is now a Durand and you will treat her as such."

Not wanting to question Antoine's words in front of our enemies, I watched their exchange with bated breath. Valentine's brows shot up to his hairline and a small smile curled over his lips. But he didn't seem enraged, as I had thought he'd be. If anything, he seemed...pleased.

"My mistake. I had heard you had gained another human servant, but I hadn't been sure if it was true or if it was the same one I had tried to buy off of you recently." There was a bite to Valentine's words that made me want to be far, far away from him. When those brown eyes locked on my form, I couldn't repress a shiver. "If I'd known, I'd have offered more."

"She's not property you can just buy, you scum sucking, bottom feeder." Rayne shoved his seat back and slammed his hands on the table, only seconds away from crawling across it to attack Valentine.

Valentine laughed at Rayne, but turned his gaze to Antoine. "I thought you had better control of your household. Perhaps I was mistaken. Again." Those eyes, full of barely contained fury, whipped back over to me.

Aren't I lucky?

Antoine didn't rise to the bait. Adjusting his coat, Antoine walked smoothly around the room to his seat on the right side of Boris. Something that I had an inkling wasn't done on accident. Taking his seat, Antoine lounged back in his chair as if he didn't have any care in the world. But the hardness to his voice when he spoke told a different story.

"Rayne is young. I cannot be held responsible for the heightened emotions of a vampling such as himself. Especially, not one who has fallen so deeply in love with my servant."

I swallowed my gasp, my eyes darting to Rayne, who didn't bother denying it. His fists were clenched on the table and if his jaw got any tighter, he'd break it. Those amber eyes though, when they fell to my face and softened, I knew it was true.

Rayne loved me.

A clap of hands to my right, and a low chuckle followed by a dreamy sigh, jerked all of our attention to the head of the table. Boris grinned from ear to ear as he took in the scene before him. "Ah, young love. Is there anything so sweet? So exciting? I remember the first time I fell in love. Of course, I was human then, but still, there's really nothing quite like it. Don't you think, Theresa?"

Theresa pulled her eyes away from Wynn long enough to meet her master's gaze. With a small smile and a nod, Theresa murmured, "Of course, master. The greatest of things." My other masters—Wynn, Marcus, Allister, and Drake—were silent in their observation of the events around them. Either they were better at pretending to keep it together than I was, or they really weren't affected. A quick glance to the fork in Drake's hand, which had been bent in half, made me bet on the former.

"And what about you, my dear?"

My head swiveled back to Boris. "What?"

Boris gave me a large, razor-sharp grin before gesturing to Rayne. "Do you return the young lad's affections?"

My mouth dried up and I searched the table for some kind of direction. I looked anywhere but at Rayne, who was stiffer than the dead. How did I answer a question like that? And in front of everyone after I had just had hot vampire sex with Antoine moments ago?

Was I with Antoine now? Was I allowed to even have feelings for Rayne? Up until a half hour ago, I didn't think Antoine wanted anything to do with me. Did I love Rayne? I cared about him and the rest of them. Some more than others. But did I?

I didn't know how to answer that question, not with the eyes of nine others on me—well, eight, since Theresa didn't give a shit and was still staring at Wynn as if he had hung the moon. How could someone be so in love with someone where they don't even care if the feeling is reciprocated?

"Well, dear, we're all waiting to hear your answer," Boris prompted me and I licked my lips and tried to find some kind of answer to give. I felt lightheaded.

"W-Water." I cleared my throat and searched around the empty table. "Can I get some water, please?"

Boris's eyes narrowed but then he snapped his fingers. "Bring Miss Durand a glass of water." Fauns, the housekeeper, appeared next to me with a water glass seconds later, placing it before me then disappearing back into the kitchen.

Not wasting a second, I picked up the glass and downed its contents. My eyes closed as the cool water quenched my dry throat and gave me much needed seconds to gather my thoughts.

This had to be a trap. Why else would they want to know about my feelings so badly? Once I sat my cup down, I tried to give Antoine some kind of signal with my eyes. A 'tell me what the fuck to say' signal that he clearly wasn't tuned in to, because he simply continued to act bored. Out of ideas, I turned my eyes to Rayne.

I don't know what to do. I pushed those thoughts at him, knowing he could hear me. *This is a trap and I know if I answer either way, we're in trouble.*

Rayne inclined his head before turning to Antoine and Boris. "I ask permission to take Piper back to her room. She's feeling a bit out of sorts having just recently been changed and traveling a long distance. I fear for her health."

"Is that so?" Valentine arched a brow in his direction before a sly grin curled up his lips. "Or are you just looking for a way to get out of the spotlight? Come now, boy. Surely, you can tell she belongs to your master. You cannot simply—"

"Valentine." The single word from Boris's mouth caused Valentine to clam up so fast that I almost thought it was funny. Almost. "Let the young ones have their secrets. All the good ones have a way of getting out on their own."

Now that didn't sound ominous. But far be it from me to look a gift horse in the mouth. I barely got to my feet before Rayne was at my side. He offered me his arm and I slowly took it, ducking my head down so as not to have to meet anyone else's gaze.

As we walked around the table, Boris called out, "I hope you feel better, Miss Durand. We wouldn't want you to miss out on all the fun."

The kitchen door opened, and a naked man and woman appeared. My eyes widened and I almost swallowed my tongue as they sat a small step stool near the table. They walked on top of the surface, moving the centerpiece out of the way, before they laid down on top of the table.

We kept walking but my head turned to watch as the vampires at the table picked up a limb. When they bit down, the humans didn't even so much as flinch. If anything, they moaned at being fed on. The scene disappeared as we moved around the corner, before I broke my neck trying to see the table.

"Come on," Rayne murmured. "You don't want to see what happens next. Trust me." I swallowed hard and nodded.

"Thank you, by the way. For that back there." I gestured my head toward the way we came.

Rayne bobbed his head. "No problem. I'm sorry they put you on the spot like that."

I pretended to focus on walking up the stairs in my dress rather than answering his unspoken question. I still didn't know a hundred percent what my answer was, but if I was going to tell anyone it would be him, and not a room full of people.

"So..." Rayne cleared his throat and stopped on the landing. "What they said, you know, back there..." He ducked his head, avoiding my gaze.

"Don't worry about it." I waved my hands between us, trying to clear the air. I pulled in my lower lip, chewing on it as I wrapped my arms around my waist and shivered.

"Cold?" Rayne asked, appearing grateful for the change of subject.

I gave a weak smile. "Yeah, a bit. I kind of miss the Lolita outfit. At least it had layers." I gestured down to the thin material of my dress with a laugh.

Rayne chuckled but his eyes roamed over my form, growing more appreciative by the second. Turning from him toward my room, or I guess Antoine's room, I kept a few feet between us. "So, Boris seems..."

"Terrifying? Fucked up? A bit loose in the head?" Rayne offered up with a sideways smirk.

"I was going to say peculiar but yeah, all of those." I dropped my arms and let them hang next to me as we walked. Our hands brushed each other as we seemed to migrate toward one another. With my emotions all kinds of twisted up, I should have stopped it, but when Rayne took my hand and laced it with his, I didn't.

I liked the feel of his hand in mine. I liked him. And while I might not love him now, I felt like could eventually. I just needed the right motivation for it.

"Rayne." I turned to him as we stopped in front of Antoine's room. His eyes locked with mine, those amber orbs with flecks of gold and brown in them I wished I could recreate. I'd wear it as a necklace around my neck so I could look at it any time I wanted to.

To my horror, Rayne's lips ticked up at the edges. "You like my eyes that much?"

With a growl, I released his hand and shoved at his chest. "Stop reading my mind."

"Stop being so easy to read," Rayne countered, grabbing my wrists and pulling me close. My chest pressed against the front of his button-down shirt, the fabric causing a delightful friction against my nipples.

"I can't help it," I muttered, so mortified I couldn't meet his gaze. He heard me extolling about his eyes. What am I? A schoolgirl?

"So, it's okay for me to listen in when you need help, but not when you're complimenting me? How's that fair?" Rayne teased, brushing my hair away from my face before settling his hand on my hip.

"That's different," I argued, shifting away from him so I could at least pretend that we weren't both turned on beyond measure. It was a little hard to forget when his bulge was poking me in the hip.

Rayne watched me for a moment, not pulling me back to him. Then, his voice lowered as he reached a hand out to lift my chin up. "I haven't been searching your brain for the answer, if that's what you're worried about."

I didn't have to ask what he was talking about. It was on both of our minds. I knew it. He knew it. I grinned up at him. "Well, too bad, I had been hoping you could tell me. 'Cause I sure as hell don't know what I'm doing here." I shrugged and crossed my arms over my chest in a feeble attempt to hide.

"It's alright, Piper." Rayne's voice became all raspy and bedroom-like, making me want to rub up against him once more. "I'm not going to make you choose. None of us will. It'd be a long eternity if we did. And nothing gets more tiring than a grudge. That's why most of us vampires don't have any."

I snorted. "Except Valentine, it seems."

Rayne's lips quirked up on one side. "Except him. He wouldn't be happy unless he was pissed at someone."

"And you?" I couldn't help but ask. "What makes you happy?"

"Right now?" Rayne arched a brow and scanned my body once more. The heat of his gaze making me shiver for a completely different reason this time. "Seeing you like this."

A sudden recklessness filled me and my eyes darted down the hallway. With no one around, I took a single step, closing the distance between us, and curled my hand into the front of Rayne's shirt before jerking his mouth to mine.

The redhead wasted no time wrapping his arms around me. His hands curled around my hips, shifting down low until he cupped my butt, pulling me against the hard bulge in his pants. My fingers sought out the tangles of his hair as I fought to claim his mouth with mine. A low moan escaped his mouth as I suckled on his tongue.

Without warning, Rayne pushed me back, releasing my mouth. He swiped a hand over his lips and shook his head. "We can't. Not here. Not out in the open like this."

I breathed heavily, confusion filling me. "Why not? Does your master have something against sharing?"

Rayne made a disgusted face that almost made me feel offended, but then he followed it up by saying, "Not as a whole, but he's playing some kind of game. I don't know what. I'm not sure if this is a good idea right now."

Tired of Boris getting to say what goes on in my life or theirs, I walked backward away from Rayne with a teasing smile. "Didn't Antoine say we needed to show a united force?"

"Yes," Rayne drawled out slowly, his eyes watching me like a predator watches its prey.

I reached a hand behind my neck and gave the tie a little tug. Rayne sucked in a hard breath when my breasts became exposed to his hungry gaze. "Then what better way than to unite...over and over again."

Rayne growled low and rushed toward me. I let out a cry of delight as I ran the rest of the way to his bedroom. My fingers curled around the doorknob just as he came in behind me, pulling my back against his front. "You are a bad, bad girl, Miss Billings." He leaned down and nipped at my neck, right where Antoine's bite was, making me gasp.

My hand reached back to keep his mouth against my neck as I muttered, "Haven't you heard? I'm a Durand now."

Chapter 9

Rayne

STAYING OUT OF PIPER'S head was harder when I was touching her, and I wouldn't stop doing that. Not now that I had permission to.

"Rayne," Piper gasped, and I heard my name both out loud and in her head as my mouth closed around her nipple. I pressed her farther into the mattress, climbing up on my knees to straddle her.

Beautiful. She was so beautiful spread out on my bed like this. Her blonde hair fanned around her head like a halo. Her pink lips swollen and puckered from my

109

kisses. The only thing that would make it better was if we were in my real bed and not at our master's home.

"You know," I whispered against her skin, moving from one breast to the other, making her gasp and cry out. "I imagined this differently."

Piper huffed out a laugh. "Did you now? And what did you imagine?"

Trailing my lips down between the valley of her breasts, I stopped briefly to tease her hip bones before shifting to grip the bottom of her dress. With a single tear of fabric, I had it off of her and on the floor in seconds, leaving her in a pair of plain white panties. Those were gone next and I couldn't wait to taste her moist heat.

"Darren is going to be so pissed at you," Piper warned, before arching her back, her eyes rolling up into her head.

I grinned against her folds as her nails dug into my hair, pulling me closer to her wet, warm center. I lapped at her until she cried out and shook beneath me. I bared my fangs, brushing them against the inside of her thigh, making her suck in a breath.

My eyes met hers before her thoughts hit my mind.

Do it.

I sank my fangs into her skin, the hot rush of her essence filling my mouth as my finger found her tight bundle of nerves once more. This was it. This was about as close as a vampire could get to someone they loved without being bound to them. One step further would be biting her while I was inside of her, but I just couldn't pull myself away from the delicious temptation between her thighs. The blood here was the sweetest during sex. So hot and full of need. I could almost feel her emotions just from drinking her blood and I could almost pretend it was me she had bonded to and not Antoine.

I pushed that thought away, not wanting to ruin the moment. When Piper cried out again, I released her, not wanting to take too much too soon after Antoine had bitten her. The last thing I wanted was for her to end up in the hospital from blood loss. Valentine and Boris didn't need any more ammunition against us.

Sliding my tongue along the wound until it sealed beneath my mouth, I sat up to peer down at Piper, checking she was still breathing. She dreamily stared up at me, her chest heaving up and down as she came down from her high.

"You vampires are going to ruin me for any other man," she joked, stroking a hand down my arm.

I leaned over her and brushed my nose against hers. "Good. Because I, for one, don't plan to ever let you go."

"Oh really?" Piper arched a brow at me, and I had a second to catch a stray thought—*my turn*—before I was pushed onto my back with Piper straddling me. "Maybe I don't want to let you go. Have you ever thought about that?"

I grinned up at her, my hands smoothing over her hips as she adjusted herself on top of me. "I'm good with that."

When Piper sank down onto my cock, I swore I saw heaven. Or maybe I was just so in love with her I couldn't see straight and I was delirious. Either way, I couldn't be happier than in this very moment. I reveled in the feel of her wrapped tightly around me as she moved up and down my cock, and the little sounds she made of pure pleasure, which only spurred my own orgasm on. When we came together, it felt like I was standing in the sun for the first time in decades. Joyful and painful and just this side of too much, but I wouldn't give it up for anything in the world. Not even if Boris himself came barging into the room this very second.

"What's that look for?" Piper asked with a coy smile.

"Nothing." I shook my head, my hand stroking up and down her back.

"None of that now." She smacked my chest with her small hand. "I can't read your mind. You have to give me something."

I peered up at her softly. "I'm just...happy."

"Oh."

My lips ticked up at the edges. "Oh? That's all you have? Oh?"

She wiggled on top of me and I grunted in response, feeling myself getting hard once more. Before she could shift off of me, I flipped us, thrusting my cock farther into her.

"Ah, Rayne, no fair." Her legs wrapped around my waist as I moved inside of her.

"What can I say?" I smirked down at her, thrusting an even more powerful stroke. "I play dirty."

Piper laughed until my thrusts caused her laughter to turn to moans and I drove us both into oblivion.

A little while later, when Piper was fast asleep in my bed, I heard a voice inside my head. *We need to talk.* Recognizing the thought as Antoine's, I slid out of bed. I pulled on my pants and shirt as I stared lovingly down at Piper. The moonlight pouring in from the windows made her creamy skin look like it was glowing where the sheets didn't cover her. When I leaned down to kiss her forehead, she let out a small sigh and snuggled deeper into my bed.

Reluctant to leave her, but knowing Antoine wouldn't give me much of a choice, I padded across my bedroom and into the hallway. There, Drake and Allister were coming out of their rooms as well. Both were only in pajama pants, our house sigil visible on their chests, they took one look at my disheveled appearance and smirked.

"Fuck off," I told them, before walking toward Antoine's room.

"What?" Drake teased, throwing an arm around my shoulders. "It's not our fault you didn't wash your activities off before coming to the meeting."

"So?" I shoved him off of me with a scowl. "What I do in my private time is that, private."

Allister snorted, crossing his arms over his bare chest. "Coming from the guy who doesn't know the definition of it."

Drake chuckled. "He has a point."

"I don't care," I countered, and shoved open Antoine's door. "And if you value your nuts, you'll leave it alone."

The second Drake walked into Antoine's room, he announced, "Rayne finally screwed Piper."

"Geez, took you long enough." Wynn clucked his tongue from the couch where he sat in a pair of silk pants and a button up shirt. Of course, he'd be dressed up for this meeting.

I shot the lazy vampire a glare before taking my place on the arm of the couch. "What's this about?" I asked Antoine, who leaned against the post of his bed.

Antoine didn't answer but waited until everyone was seated and accounted for. The twins stood over by the wardrobe, while Marcus barred the door like usual as if he were guarding us from leaving. Darren sat on the bed, prim and proper in his white and blue striped pajamas.

I admit, I tried to listen to Antoine's thoughts. I wanted to know if he was pissed that Piper and I had slept together, but as usual I only heard what he wanted

115

me to hear and right now he didn't want me to hear anything.

"This situation is worse than we could have imagined." Antoine stared off into space as if none of us were really there. "This isn't just some test to see if we have strayed from Boris's lifestyle."

"Well, of course not," Drake scoffed, brushing his thumb across his nose. "We know what this is about. Valentine. He threw a hissy fit 'cause he couldn't steal Piper as his new toy and now wants us to pay."

"True." Antoine nodded, finally meeting our gazes. "But it's about more than that. I believe that he, Boris, is trying to bring us back into the fold."

"What?" I straightened, my eyes widening with surprise. "He can't do that. Can he do that?" I glanced around the room, my heart pounding in my chest.

"He can try," Drake growled, his whole form tightening up.

A sick feeling twisted in my stomach and I had to take slow, shallow breaths to keep from upchucking or passing out or both. While I focused on that, everyone's thoughts became a chaotic blur, filling my head until I couldn't pick one out from the other.

"Quiet." Antoine's voice rang out through the room, the force of his power instantly quieting the space and the voices in my head. Everyone looked to Antoine for guidance. He'd led us out of hell, so if anyone could keep us out of here, it would be him.

"Now, I understand your concern." Antoine's eyes drifted over to me briefly. His thoughts a soothing comfort to ease the rumbling turmoil in my chest. "I promised you years ago when we left this place that we would never be under our master's thumb again. We are our own house. Coming here was a diplomatic choice, but it was that...a choice. Boris might have made us, but he does not own us. Not anymore." He paused for a moment, his face clouding over with darkness. "We paid that price."

Wynn snorted. "Ten times over."

"Precisely." Antoine inclined his head.

None of us spoke for a moment. I didn't need to peek into their heads to know what they were thinking, because I was thinking it too.

That day when we first requested to leave our master's house and become our own was one that left a scar on each of us. Boris didn't just demand payment for

117

one of us, but all of us. Each one of us had to pay their bit of blood and flesh, even a part of our sanity, to be free. The fact that any of us came back here after what we went through to get out was laughable. But I guess that proved how much we all cared about Piper and keeping Valentine as far away from her as possible.

Allister stepped into the middle of the room, his arms tight across his chest as he spoke. "Vampire law states that once abjured, our master cannot command us back into his home. We are here because we have made it so, not the other way around. Which means he cannot force us to stay. We have to want to," Allister finished with a confident grin.

"Pfft, bloody likely that's going to happen," Wynn snorted and shifted in place. "I'd sooner fall on a stake than stay here."

"Agreed." Antoine nodded and the rest of joined him.

"So..." I sighed, a bit more relaxed about the conversation and where it was headed. "What other surprises do you think our dear old daddy has in store for us?"

Chapter 10
Piper

I AWOKE WITH A start. Lifting my head up from my pillow, I scanned the room. This wasn't my room. The sheet in my hand covered my naked body and suddenly it all came rushing back to me.

I flushed and rubbed my thighs together in remembrance before turning slowly in bed. I'd expected to see a redheaded vampire next to me, but what I got was an empty bed. My hand touched the wrinkled spot on the sheets, but it was cool.

Oh. Duh. Vampire.

Of course, it was going to be cool. It still didn't answer my question though. Where was Rayne?

Sliding my legs over the side of the bed, I pulled the sheets off and around me like a toga. When my feet touched the cool wooden floors, I shivered.

Clothes. I needed clothes.

I blindly searched for the light on the nightstand and clicked it on. The room, once cast in the dim moonlight, gained an orange glow. Now able to somewhat see, I easily found my dress from dinner. Unfortunately, it was a bit worse for wear. Looked like I wasn't putting that back on.

My eyes drifted over to Rayne's dresser and my lips ticked up into a smirk. I shouldn't. Still, my feet padded over to the dresser and I pulled open one drawer, and then the another, until I found Rayne's shirts.

Pulling out a t-shirt, I dropped the sheet and dragged the shirt over my head. Since Rayne and I were about the same height, the shirt wasn't long enough to cover my ass. I searched for my underwear, which was thankfully still intact. Putting them on under the shirt, I searched Rayne's other drawers for some sweatpants or something. Finding a pair of drawstring pants, I tugged them over my legs, but had to tie them tight to keep them from falling.

There. Now to find Rayne.

I ducked into his bathroom and frowned when he wasn't there either. I relieved my bladder and washed my hands. Before leaving the bathroom, I glanced toward the bedroom door. Maybe he went to get something to eat? It technically was still his daytime hours, right?

My feet made light sounds as I walked to the door and slowly twisted the doorknob. For a second, I thought it might be locked, but then with a sigh it opened. I shook my head at my silliness and then peeked my head out into the hallway.

The halls of Boris's home were intimidating in the daytime, and at night, they were downright scary. With only a few walls sconces turned on, the hallway was all doom and gloom. Reminiscent of the days the castle was new. Looking both ways, I chewed on my lower lip as I contemplated searching for Rayne. A glance at the bedside clock said it was just after two in the morning. I'd left my phone back in Antoine's room along with the rest of my stuff. If anything, I should go check in. Make sure my mother hadn't blown up my phone after their surprise visit.

That's doubtful after what Antoine did to them.

It was still a bit creepy that Antoine could control human minds so easily. The way he had handled my parents with ease was both impressive and frightening. It made me wonder if he'd ever done it to me. Of course, it wasn't like I would know even if he had. Still, it was something to ask the vampire later.

Scrounging up my courage, I stepped out into the hallway. It took me a second to remember I was in Rayne's room, so my room was in the opposite direction. A girl could get lost in this place with all the rooms and doors looking the same. I was lucky I'd had a guide so far. I didn't dare try and explore on my own. Besides getting lost, there was the fact that I was a human in a vampire's domain. With my luck, I'd walk right into Boris's bedroom. Or worse. Valentine's. A shiver ran down my back at the thought. No thank you.

Walking as quickly as I could down the hallway, I tried my best to keep calm and not jump at every noise. Vampires could smell fear, as well as hear my racing heart. The less appealing I was to them, the less likely they would come after me. Or at least, that was what I hoped.

I reached my room without incident, and I let out a long and heavy sigh before reaching for the doorknob. My hand paused before it reached the handle. There were voices inside. I leaned closer to the wood. That wasn't just Antoine and Darren. The whole group was in there.

Were they having a meeting without me? Annoyance filled my chest. If they were going to make plans behind my back, then they didn't really trust me the way they said. Didn't they say before that since I was the one Valentine and Boris were going gaga over, that I should be in on the plans? So much for that. Apparently, I was good enough to fuck but not to include in important decisions.

I tried to hear what they were saying but the words were garbled. One thing I knew for sure was they were arguing. Something had their panties in a twist. Was it me? Were they fighting over me?

"It's rude to eavesdrop, you know," a smooth, silky voice whispered behind me. I practically jumped a mile high and barely contained the screech that wanted to come out of me. Spinning in place, I came face to face with a smirking Valentine.

Great. Just who I was trying to avoid.

Crossing my arms over my chest—my braless chest for that matter—I scowled at the vampire. "I wasn't eavesdropping. I was waiting for them to finish so I could go in." I tried not to shift in place. I didn't want Valentine to know how much his presence bothered me. If I'd learned anything from Darren and the others, it was that Valentine was a typical bully. If he knew he bothered me, then he would be even more inclined to find reasons to mess with me.

"Then go in," Valentine taunted with a sly grin.

"I will." But then I didn't move. I didn't want to be out in the hallway with Valentine, but I also didn't want to go in there with the guys. If they'd been talking about me, then they'd know for sure I had been listening in. If they hadn't been, then I'd feel like an idiot. Also, they'd smell that Rayne and I had sex, and that's not something I was ready to face yet.

As if reading my mind, Valentine sniffed the air, his nostrils flaring, and a snarl curled his lips to reveal his fangs.

"You've let another one defile you, I see. What should I expect from a little human slut like you?" I flinched and backstepped as Valentine moved in closer.

"T-That's none of your business," I snapped, cursing myself for stuttering. "What I do with my masters is between us."

"Ah, but you have it all wrong." Valentine braced his hands on either side of me, leaning in until he was only inches away. It almost seemed like he might kiss me, but then at the last second, he turned his head, brushing his lips down my cheek, his nose sniffing along my neck. He traced the line of the scar on my neck where Antoine had bound me to him, and growled, "I really wish you hadn't done that."

"What?" I answered, trying to get him talking and not focused on my skin. On my blood. Why weren't the guys coming? Couldn't they hear us out here? Fuck me for choosing the coward's way out. Now, Valentine would suck me dry right outside their bedroom door and there was nothing I could do about it.

Valentine huffed and tossed his strawberry blond hair a bit like a horse would. "You think that his mark will protect you? He's nothing." Valentine's hands drifted down to grab the sides of my head, his eyes locking with mine. "Antoine's power is nothing compared to mine. I could take you right now, make you mine, even with his mark on your neck. In your blood."

The longer I stared into Valentine's hazelnut colored eyes, the more I believed what he said. Antoine was weak. Valentine was strong. He should be my master. Not someone as unworthy as Antoine Durand.

Valentine released my head with a satisfied smile. "Yes, that's it pet. Tell me, who's your master?"

I opened my mouth to answer him, it was clearly him, but then Antoine's voice rose above the others behind me in the room separated from me by a wooden door. No. It wasn't Valentine. Antoine. Antoine was my master. Wait. Fuck that. Anger billowed up inside me, making me grind my teeth. Faking a sweet dopey smile, I reached up and placed my hands on Valentine's shoulders. Pretending to press up on my toes to kiss him, I pulled one leg back and shoved it up with all my might. My knee found its soft target and Valentine's eyes went wide. Clutching his damaged goods, Valentine stumbled back from me with a groan.

"You-you bitch," he croaked out, and tried to grab me while holding himself.

Jumping away from him, I laughed. "Good to know that even vampires can be taken down with the right motivation."

However, my laughter died off as I realized that vampires recovered far faster than men did. Valentine's eyes glowed with an ethereal evil light, and he bared his fangs seconds before he came at me. I let out a high-pitched scream and curled back into the door. If I was smart, I'd have run, but apparently I was stupid in the face of danger. Not surprising with my track record. When Antoine had caught me trying to leave the manor after I found out what they were, I hadn't been smart then either. If I survived this, I'd have to make a conscious effort to change that.

Valentine's hands latched on to my shoulders and jerked me to him. His fangs sank into my neck. The agonizing pain of my flesh ripping caused me to let out another bloodcurdling scream, but this time Valentine was ready for me. His hand clamped down over my mouth, pushing against my face until I could barely breathe, let alone make a sound.

I thought for sure that I was going to die right here in the hallway tonight. Tears burned my eyes as they trailed down my face and I realized that no one was coming for me. No one was going to save me. If they were, they would have done been here if they had heard me. Why, oh, why hadn't I just faced the embarrassment and gone into Antoine's room? Why did I have to taunt the evil vampire instead?

Valentine's grip on me tightened as he gulped down my blood, and I was beginning to get lightheaded. I was becoming unsteady on my feet when all of a sudden, there was a loud curse and Valentine was ripped away from me, taking a good chunk of my neck with him. My legs went out from under me, but I didn't hit the ground. Strong arms wrapped around me and the scent of jasmine and thunder filled my nose before everything went black.

Chapter 11

Antoine

"THIS IS NOT A negotiation," I snarled, frustration filling my voice. "No one is going to sacrifice themselves to save the others. We are going to all make it out together, with Piper." My eyes moved over the room, meeting the gazes of my blood brothers. Each of us had a reason never to want to come back to this place, but all of us came back for her. If that wasn't a testament to how much we had come to care about the little human woman, then nothing was.

"I'm not saying anyone should sacrifice themselves," Drake countered with a frown, as he leaned forward from where he had taken a seat on my bed. The same bed I had tasted Piper on just a few short hours ago. Against my will, my eyes slid over to Rayne. Piper had slept with Rayne. That much was clear. The scent of sex still clung to Rayne's skin and the sweet scent of Piper tinged my nose. It overrode any other scent in the room. A part of me wanted to tell Rayne to go back to his room and shower, but that would be admitting I cared if Piper slept with Rayne and I wasn't about to do that.

"Then what are you saying?" Rayne asked, with an irritated scowl. "I'm not playing the puppet for him anymore. I won't. I can't." A dark shadow crossed behind Rayne's amber eyes.

I understood where Rayne was coming from. As the youngest of those our master had changed, Rayne had been the most popular with the other vampires. Especially those who preferred young boys. If it wasn't forbidden to change children into vampires, then I was sure some of our master's friends would have done it already. It wouldn't surprise me if they did in secret. Though, the punishment was death by starvation.

Oh, we could die alright. In some of the most grotesque ways possible. Sunlight burned if we were exposed to it for too long, a stake to the heart or a knife to the neck was the quickest and most merciful way to kill us, and the longest and most drawn out was starvation.

We wouldn't die after a few days of not eating. No, that would have been preferable to the hell that we went through. A vampire, if unfed, desiccated...slowly. Each day was a burning, gasping need for blood until you were a rampaging animal ready to feed on anything that was within biting distance, including yourself. Eventually, you become so weak, that you just lay there with the moisture sucking from your skin as you become not much more than a living husk. It wasn't a pretty sight. I'd seen it a time or two in my lifetime, and it wasn't something you easily forgot.

Our master liked to punish his creations with starvation. I'd been locked away for weeks at a time dying but not dying, all because I dared to displease him in some way. He always let me out of course—I was his favorite after all—but

131

those days felt like an eternity. However, it was nothing compared to what Marcus has endured at the hand of our master.

My eyes flicked in the direction of my sentinel, the logical one of my brothers. Which was surprising, since at one time he would have been called the crazy one. Now, he was the brother I went to when I needed an unbiased or unemotionally based opinion. Sometimes, though, Marcus could be too logical, as was the case with Piper. I hoped I wasn't putting her in danger by just having him around.

Seconds before a sharp tang of blood filled my nose, terror ripped through my chest. Piper. I froze. A quick look around the room showed that the rest of them had smelled it too. Just as Rayne murmured, "Piper," I was slamming the bedroom door open.

My heart lodged in my throat at the sight before me. Piper was clutched in the arms of Valentine. His filthy fangs were inside her neck as tears ran down her face. How had I not heard them? We hadn't been arguing that much for me to miss this, had we?

Before I could think, my feet were moving and I slammed into Valentine, ripping him away from Piper. Piper started to collapse to the floor, but Wynn was there in time to catch her, leaving Valentine to me. I snarled and bared my fangs at the bastard who smelled of Piper's sweet blood. "What the hell do you think you are doing?"

"Why, tasting our girl." Valentine smiled and licked the blood dripping from his lips. He didn't seem at all concerned by the fact that I had him by the throat. He really should be. I tightened my fingers around his neck until he winced.

I could hear the others crowding around us, whispering warnings of caution, but I ignored them. The protectiveness in my chest burned for me to seek vengeance for Piper.

"She is not *our* girl. Piper is mine," I roared at Valentine, my nails slicing into his skin until his blood slid down his neck and stained his pristine shirt. I had always hated how clean of an eater he was, but now I was happy for it. I didn't know how I would have reacted had he been covered in Piper's life source.

Even so, I was tempted to squeeze until Valentine's smug head popped off his shoulders. I was two seconds away from doing it too, but a heavy, familiar hand landed on my shoulder. My eyes shifted

133

from Valentine to the large form next to me and I clenched my jaw. "Stay out of this, Marcus."

"Not here." Marcus's rumbling voice filled the hallway, even though he was murmuring. My eyes locked back onto Valentine's who wasn't smiling anymore. My lips ticked up in satisfaction. Marcus's hand tightened on my shoulder, and I snarled at him.

"Marcus is right, Antoine." Allister took up the other side of me, but didn't touch me. I could feel his words of persuasion slide over me. He wasn't as powerful as me, but it did make me pause.

"Stop," I growled in warning. "Or I'll kill you next."

"Come now, Antoine. We're all upset." Drake stood by his brother and tried to reason with me. "No one wants to see this putz pay more than us, but this isn't the time or place. What do you think our master will do if he sees we've killed one of our own in his home?"

Dammit. He had a point.

My eyes narrowed on Valentine and with one, last snarl and a huff, I shoved him away from me. Valentine grabbed his throat, his eyes locked on me, and for a second I could see him wanting to come at me. Then his gaze went to my brothers who were crowded around me—except Wynn, who still had Piper in his arms behind us.

"You're going to regret this, Durand." Valentine backed away from us and down the hall, but not without swiping a finger along his lower lip and popping it into his mouth in an exaggerated manner. With a hum and a pop of his digit, Valentine purred, "Delicious."

This time, it was Rayne who started for the asshole, but he was easily restrained by Drake and Allister. All of our eyes watched until Valentine disappeared into the darkness, and then when his scent was far enough away, we relaxed and turned back to Piper.

"How is she?" Rayne rushed to her side, kneeling where she lay on the ground in Wynn's arms.

Piper could almost be sleeping. Her eyes were closed, and her chest rose and fell in an even pattern. Except she wasn't sleeping. At least, not peacefully. She had passed out from the blood loss. There was nothing normal about that.

In addition, I could feel Piper in my chest, weak and fragile. At least she wasn't afraid anymore. I had tried my best to push her emotions away all day. Especially earlier when she was with Rayne. Sometimes, having human servants was like having someone else in your head. It made me have new sympathy for Rayne and his abilities. Piper must have been really afraid to get through the walls I had put up to keep her out. Shame and guilt filled me. It was my own selfishness that had kept me from feeling her distress earlier. If I hadn't been blocking her, then I might have known Valentine was out here with her and he wouldn't have gotten his dirty fangs in her.

"Is she okay?" Drake asked, standing over Wynn with a curious but worried frown. "She's not going to die, is she?"

"Don't be an idiot," Rayne growled, shoving past him to kneel by Wynn. "You've been a vampire for how long? You can clearly see she's not going to die. Plus..." He trailed off, his lips tilting downward. "I can hear her thoughts. She's not dead."

Drake snorted and shook his head. "Well then, oh annoying one, what is she thinking."

"That you both need to keep your mouths shut," I snarled at the two bickering vampires. "We don't need to draw any more attention to us than we already have."

"Agreed." Wynn nodded and moved to stand. "We need to get her inside before we attract the whole household with her blood."

Everyone took a deep breath and let out a needy sigh before we realized what we'd all done. Clearing my throat, I tried to reach for her, but Wynn held tight.

"It's fine. I've got her." Wynn brushed passed me to the bedroom door, which was still ajar from when we had all rushed out before. We filed in one by one with Marcus bringing up the rear and closing the door behind us.

Darren stood by the bed with a glass of water and bandages. My lips ticked up on their own. Always the prepared one. Pushing that thought away, I focused more on Piper. Wynn laid her down on the bed and turned her head to the side. She groaned and flinched away from his touch, and no wonder, the side of her neck was a mess. Valentine hadn't been just eating to feed, but to hurt. It made the fact that he hadn't gotten any on his clothes even more astounding.

137

My anger bubbled up inside me like a simmering pot of water just seconds from boiling over. I couldn't believe I had let this happen.

"How could we let this happen?" Allister parroted my thoughts from the other side of the bed, sitting down on the mattress and picking up Piper's hand like it would break any moment. "We're supposed to keep her safe and we didn't even know she was in trouble right outside our door?"

Wynn grabbed a washcloth from Darren and proceeded to clean the wound. If we'd been just a second later, Valentine would have ripped her throat out. I tore my eyes away from her, the sight the blood spurring my disgust instead of my hunger for once.

A loud thud followed by splintering wood filled the room. Drake huffed and growled, his hands full of the wooden post he'd just broken off at the foot of the bed. "I say we stake the bastard. Wait until dawn and stake him in his sleep. I have the weapon right here."

Rayne snorted. "And then what? Our master would be on us in an instant. We'd never leave this place, let alone alive."

"Rayne's right." I nodded, taking slow, deep breaths to clear my head. "We cannot act rashly right now. That is what Valentine wants, and for all we know what our master wants. No." I paused, focusing my gaze on Piper. "What we need to do right now is make sure this never happens again. Someone must be with Piper at all times. No leaving her behind."

Rayne gave a dark chuckle. "She's not going to like that."

I shot him a look. "Well, I'm past caring what she wants in this matter. Piper is ours. We will protect her better than this. We have to."

The room sounded their agreement. Then Wynn shifted toward me on the bed. "She needs blood. Since she's your human servant..." He trailed off, letting me fill in the blanks.

Unbuttoning the cuff on my sleeve, I traded places with Wynn. I lifted my wrist to my mouth and bit down until I tasted copper. Turning my wrist toward Piper, Allister helped me lift her up without hitting her neck wound. I pressed my bloody wrist to her lips, coaxing her to open her mouth.

Piper groaned and tried to turn her head, but I tut-tutted. "You must drink,

Piper. Drink." I forced my wrist between her lips and her tongue hesitantly lashed out at the fluid filling her mouth. Her eyes snapped open and her hands grabbed my arm tightly to her, sucking down the blood like her life depended on it. And for just a moment, I realized how much I could have.

Chapter 12
Piper

MY HEAD FELT LIKE it was an overfilled water balloon just seconds away from bursting. I rolled over on the bed and moved my mouth. Ugh. Why did it taste like I'd eaten a dirty bag of pennies?

A movement to my left, followed by the mattress dipping, was my only signal that someone else was in the room. It was quiet. Too quiet. I tried to open my eyes, but they were so heavy.

"Don't move just yet," a low, sultry voice I knew too well told me, and then

Wynn's hand stroked down my back. "You've lost a lot of blood."

Blood? Why did I lose blood? A sharp pain in my neck made all the memories coming rushing back.

Dinner with our creepy host. Leaving to have sex with Rayne. Having sex with Rayne. Then waking to find myself alone. Only to run into Valentine.

I whimpered as the memory of his fangs sinking into my neck resurfaced, and tears slid out of my eyes and pooled beneath my cheek, wetting the pillow. My hand moved up to touch my neck where it still hurt, but it was covered in gauze.

"Shh, now." Wynn took my hand and lowered it. "You're safe. You're going to be sore, but in a few hours, you will be right as rain."

How could that be? I was sure Valentine was going to kill me. He'd taken so much blood and he just wouldn't stop. I'd tried to push him away, but he was so strong. So heavy. And it hurt so much. I had kept crying out in my head for Rayne or any of them to come but they didn't. No one did. Not until it was too late.

A finger brushed beneath my eyes where tears still fell. A shocking ripple of pleasure warmed me and pushed back some of the pain, the horror. My eyes flipped open to meet Wynn's startlingly blue eyes. He peered down at me, not with lust, but with concern and warmth. Dressed in silk pajamas, he seemed perfectly at ease at my side. I reached for his hand, drawing it to my cheek. I wanted that feeling. I needed it. It had to be better than the madness filling my mind.

"You should rest," Wynn insisted, trying to slip his hand out of mine to stand. "Antoine's blood will kick in any minute now, and it'll work faster if you are well rested."

I held tight to his hand, even though I knew he could pull it away if he really wanted to, but he didn't. "Please. Please don't stop. It hurts...so much," I choked out, and the tears poured more freely than ever. Wynn settled back down on the mattress and pressed his hand to my cheek once more. The pleasurable feeling spread through me again. It wasn't the raging desire of lust I knew Wynn could induce, but instead just the heady warmth that came from the preamble of a kiss, a look. That very thing that made you think you could fall in love. It was a far cry better than feeling like a victim. A chew toy for that...that...monster. Dammit. I was usually better at insults, but I couldn't even muster up the strength to call Valentine a name that really described how horrible he really was.

"Better?"

My lashes fluttered to look at Wynn once more and I nodded. "Yeah. Thanks." I shifted and tried to sit up, but I felt heavier than usual. As if gravity was pulling me down until my head was on the pillow again. I sighed in frustration. "This sucks."

Wynn quirked a smile. "I can imagine. Here." He turned and picked up a glass off the nightstand. A quick look past him told me I was in Antoine's room. Well, at least I made it where I was going. Even if it wasn't the way I had planned. I let out a sad, pathetic laugh, making Wynn arch a brow. "Nothing. Just being morbid."

Bringing the water glass to me, Wynn helped me sit up to take a drink. "Please do tell. I would love nothing else more than to hear your morbid thoughts."

After I quenched my thirst, it was my turn to raise my eyebrows. "Really?" Then I realized how silly I was being. "Oh, of course you do. You're a vampire. Morbid is kind of your thing, isn't it?"

Shaking his head with a laugh, Wynn placed the glass back on the nightstand. "Being a vampire has nothing to do with it. I know quite a few vampires who can't stand the sight of blood, let alone death."

"What?" My mouth fell open in shock. "How does that work?"

Lifting a shoulder and dropping it, Wynn turned back to me with a smile. "From what I understand, they have their cook mix the blood into smoothies and other edibles. It helps them pretend they are at least a bit human, even if they are anything but."

I nodded or tried to. The movement pulled on my neck wound and made me wince. "I thought vampire blood healed faster than this. When Rayne broke my wrist, I didn't heal this slowly. Or it didn't feel that way."

"You don't seem to understand the gravity of your situation, Piper," Wynn murmured, his eyes lowering to the bedspread. "You almost died."

Licking my lips, I reached out and placed my hand on top of his, curling my fingers around it until he looked up. "I know. I could feel it. I don't know how, but

145

there was something my chest telling me that I was going to die, and I was so scared. None of you came and I swore you would come." My lip quivered and I had to catch my breath before I started to hyperventilate.

Wynn drew me up and into his arms, wrapping me up in his embrace. "Shhh, it's okay. I've got you. You'll never ever be in that situation ever again. Not while any of us are alive."

I let him rub my back and rock me back and forth like I was a child until my sobbing eased once more. With a sigh, I pulled away from Wynn's chest and stared up into his eyes. Those bright blue eyes that mesmerize me from the beginning. Without thinking, I leaned in and pressed my mouth to his pouty lips.

But Wynn didn't kiss me back.

Frowning and embarrassed as all hell, I pulled back and tucked a strand of hair behind my ear. "I'm sorry. I thought you and I... I shouldn't have assumed after everything with Antoine and Rayne." I moved to get out of his lap, but Wynn held me closer, making me look up at him in confusion.

"Piper, please don't take this as a rejection. I don't care about who else you have given your heart to." Wynn cupped the side of my face and drew me close. "I would love nothing more than to kiss you and soothe away all your fears, but you arc hurt. Now is not the time."

"But when will be? You've made this excuse before." I felt myself pouting like a toddler. "Don't you want me?"

Those ocean blue eyes filled with hot, molten desire and when he spoke next, my whole body shuddered in need. "Oh, yes. Piper. I want you greatly." Then, as if it had never happened, Wynn picked me up and sat me on the bed. Giving me a low bow, he grinned and winked. "But not until you are well. I am, if anything, a gentleman."

A scoff from the doorway pulled our attention. Antoine stood on the threshold, imposing and arrogant as ever. He still wore his dress shirt and slacks, but the top few buttons were undone, and a speckle of hair peeked out showing just a hint of the tattoo over his heart. His hands in his pockets, Antoine sauntered into the room as if he didn't have a care in the world. Except there was a tightness to his movements, a bit of a robotic likeness to it, that showed me everything was not as it seemed.

Antoine stopped in front of the desk, his eyes down as he leafed through a few papers there.

"What?" I probed, when Antoine didn't say anything.

Not lifting his head, Antoine hummed.

"What was that sound about?" I pressed with a wave of my hand and a frown. "You can't just come in here and make rude noises without explanations."

"I can't?" Antoine finally looked up, his eyes twinkling with amusement, and I swore his lips were twitching to hold back a smile.

I narrowed my eyes on him, even as Wynn simply shook his head. "No, you can't."

"Oh, so you're the master now. Are you?" The sharpness to his words, even with the playful look on his face, confused me. It made Wynn tense up, but he didn't move from the bed.

"Uh..." I glanced between the two of them, not sure what I was supposed to do. When Antoine moved, stalking toward the bed, Wynn stepped in front of him with his hands up between them.

"She's still hurt. Don't do this now." The other vampire seemed to be pleading with Antoine, but Antoine wouldn't be

148

dissuaded from whatever he was going to do. Wynn sighed, and cast me an apologetic look over his shoulder before moving to the couch. He appeared to be determined to keep an eye on me, even if he couldn't stop his brother.

"What's going on?" I hated the way my voice shook when I spoke, my gaze darting between the two vampires.

Antoine reached up and unbuttoned the buttons of his shirt, one at a time with slow, agonizing precision. My eyes followed the movements. Hypnotized by the deftness of his fingers and the delicious expanse of muscles appearing before my eyes, I didn't think I had any need to worry.

"Piper." The way Antoine said my name with such sternness and contempt made me pause. My gaze shot up to his and I licked my lips, my mouth suddenly dry. "Did you not understand how dangerous of a situation we have found ourselves in?"

My brows furrowed. "Of course. I'm not stupid. I know we're in trouble."

"Then why would you think it would be a good idea to traipse around this godforsaken place on your own? Without

149

anyone for protection? Didn't you learn anything from Valentine's last visit?"

"Why, I—"

"And did you think that you wouldn't be punished for not following orders?" Antoine stopped in front of the bed and I froze at the word punished.

"Punished? Why would you—" I gaped, and my wide eyes slid over to Wynn who only shook his head sadly before bringing them back to Antoine. "You can't be serious. I'm a grown woman. What are you going to do, send me to bed without supper?" I let out a nervous chuckle that neither of them smiled at.

"I am deadly serious, Piper." Antoine reached for me quick as lightning. Before I knew it or could even struggle, I was thrown across his lap and my ass was bare to the air. I kicked my legs and tried to roll away, but Antoine's grip was unbreakable. Finally, my eyes went to Wynn, pleading for him to help me.

"You have to understand, Piper," Wynn stroked his lower lip as he watched me, his eyes heating even as the frown on his lips deepened, "how dangerous this place and our kind can be, and the only way to make sure you don't forget is to make sure you remember."

"I'll remember. Don't you think I'll remember?" I screeched, not at all happy about being treated like a child. "I almost died. That's enough to keep me from doing it again. I promise. I won't. I promise," I finished weakly, while Antoine adjusted his grip on me as I finally gave up and stopped fighting.

Antoine's hand sat on my butt for a moment as he leaned down to speak to me. "It is not only your life that you risk when you put yourself in these situations, but ours. If one of us had killed Valentine for what he had done to you, then what do you think would have happened? Do you think our master would simply let us go? Any of us?"

I sniffed and shook my head. "No." It was true. I had barely met the master vampire, but knew already that beneath all the pleasantries, he was a vicious beast. If anyone displeased him, he wouldn't hesitate to kill them on the spot or worse.

"Believe me when I tell you, I get no joy out of this." Antoine sat back up and then lifted his hand. I held my breath as I prepared for the hit. My parents had never spanked me. I didn't know what to expect. So, when his hand sailed through the air and landed on my ass cheek with a resounding smack, I was so shocked I barely cried out. The next one Antoine landed was on the opposite cheek, and then to make it even worse, something changed about it. Changed within me. Each smack caused a stinging sensation that spread out and lingered between my thighs. My head jerked up as I heard Wynn suck in a breath.

His eyes were locked on me, his lips parted as he breathed in my scent. I didn't know what was wrong with me. I shouldn't be turned on by this. I was getting spanked for god's sake. But the way Wynn was watching me only spurred on the sensations I was feeling. After the last smack on my ass, Antoine's fingers slid between my ass cheeks until they dipped into my wetness.

"Naughty girl," Antoine murmured. "You are not supposed to enjoy your punishment. Perhaps I'll have to find something else to get my point across, but first...Wynn." Antoine's voice called out across the room, and Wynn was immediately on his feet and standing before me. "Piper doesn't seem to be getting the point of this little exercise. Suppose you can help her?"

152

Wynn let out a shuddering breath before reaching for me. Antoine fixed my pants and handed me over to Wynn. Confused and still reeling from the shocking punishment I'd enjoyed far too much, I held on to Wynn by his shirt. I wasn't sure what Antoine wanted Wynn to do, but since his particular power had a happy ending, I wasn't too worried. In fact, I was excited for it.

"Don't look so eager, lovely." Wynn smirked at me, stroking my cheek with his hand. That one caress sent a hot burn through my body. My nipples tightened into hard points and my thighs pressed tightly against each other, trying to ease the pulsing need between them.

A small, gasping moan released from my mouth and I sank against Wynn. "Are you going to punish me, Wynn?"

Antoine watched beside us, not moving from where he sat on the bed. He crossed one leg over the other and leaned back on his elbow. I'd have found his ease concerning, but I was too focused on keeping my feet on the floor and not crumbling out from under me. Wynn barely touched me. Every caress and brush of his fingers above the neckline. Nevertheless, each innocent touch

153

pushed me further and further toward the deep end, until I was just on the edge and was begging Wynn not to stop.

"Please," I gasped, my fingers tightening on his silk pajama shirt. I should have been embarrassed by how desperate I sounded, but I was too close to care. "Wynn. I'm almost there. I..."

"Stop." Antoine's voice called out, and I stared at Wynn as he slowly removed his hands from me and stepped back.

"No." My eyes widened and then jerked over to Antoine, before going back to Wynn. "No, no. You can't be serious. You can't just stop now."

Wynn didn't answer me, and I reached for him but he was too fast. He took another step back and then he was out the bedroom door, not bothering to close it behind him.

Rage and need pulsated through me as I spun on Antoine. "I can't believe you. You fucking asshole."

Antoine stared at me flatly before standing to his feet. He adjusted his pants, brushing off some invisible lint, before taking one step toward me. Brushing my hair over my shoulder, he touched the edge of the gauze, and I flinched. "Let this be a lesson to you."

I glared up at him and then in a moment of bravery, placed my hands on my hips and snapped, "I'll just get myself off when you leave then."

"No, you won't." Antoine command filled every inch of me. The resistance I thought I had to his abilities apparently wasn't working, because every cellular part of my being demanded I obeyed him.

"What are you doing to me?"

Antoine tipped my chin up, pinching it between his thumb and forefinger. "You are weak right now and have my blood coursing through you. It makes you more susceptible to my powers. Now, you will lay down and think about what you did. And while your nipples ache and your pussy begs to be stroked, you will resist. You will not cum until I say you can. Do you understand?"

I fought against the command in his voice. I fought until my jaw ached from clenching my teeth, but it was for nothing. My mouth opened on its own and a feeble, "Yes, sir," came pouring out.

"Good. Now go to bed. I will send Darren in to check on you later." He released my chin and walked toward the bedroom door, trusting me to do as he ordered.

155

Not like I had a choice.

The moment he released me, my feet moved on their own and I found myself climbing into bed. The covers brushed over my sensitive chest, making me shudder with want. I shifted my legs, trying and failing to quell the desire pounding to a beat that didn't seem to ebb, even after I laid there for thirty minutes.

It was torture. Pure torture. I'd have preferred a lashing to this, but I knew one thing for sure, I wouldn't forget myself again.

Chapter 13

Allister

GATHERED IN MY TWIN'S room, my blood brothers were quieter than usual. Each of us had something on our minds and I was willing to bet the majority of us were contemplating death. Valentine's death in particular.

"He needs to die," Drake growled, pounding his fist against his thigh where he sat at my desk.

"Now, let's not be so hasty." Antoine held a hand up. Our leader had cooled down quite a lot since our last meeting.

Still, it was surprising to hear him not agreeing with Valentine's demise.

"You just want him to get away with it?" Drake gaped, his hands waving around in agitation. "That fucker is just gonna come after her again. He won't stop. Not until she's dead."

"Drake's got a point," I interjected with a nod, shifting on my bed. "Valentine is a singular creature. Once he has a taste for someone, he won't quit."

Rayne snorted next to Wynn on the couch. "Well, he's tasted her now. If you could call what he did to her tasting. More like brutalized her."

Wynn shook his head and sighed, rubbing a hand over his face. "You guys didn't see her afterward. Piper was really shook up."

"Of course she would be." Rayne turned his head toward Wynn with a frown. "What human wouldn't be? That wasn't a feeding. He was trying to kill her." He ground his teeth, his hands tightening on his thighs. "And he'll try it again. I know it. I could hear his thoughts. It was..." He shook his head, his eyes filled with despair. "It was horrible. We can't let him touch her again." Rayne's shaggy red head lifted, his gaze locking with Antoine's. "I vote he dies."

"Here, here!" Drake pumped his fist in the air.

I sighed and lifted my hand as well. "I do too. Piper deserves justice."

"And she'll get it," Antoine countered with a stern frown. "But not by putting us in danger. If we kill Valentine, what do you think our master will do?"

Drake barked out a laugh. "Then we kill that fucker too."

A few of us chuckled nervously, but then we paused. Turning my head to Antoine, I cocked it to the side in thought. "Can we? It would solve a lot of our problems."

Antoine didn't answer right away, but then jerked his head in an upward motion. "But this is not the place to be discussing such things. There are too many ears." He swirled his finger in the air, gesturing to the walls. He was right. Who knew who could be listening, even now. There were no secrets in this house, and us planning the assassination of our master and creator was not best idea in his house.

"We need to make a plan." Drake leaned forward in the desk chair, his

159

elbows on his knees as he laced his fingers beneath his chin. "We can't do that here."

"We can't leave though," Wynn pointed out. "Not without leaving Piper vulnerable. She'd have to come with us."

"Where though?" Rayne shifted to address the group. "Where could we take her to discuss this?"

Antoine stepped into the center of the room. "Our master will no doubt want to throw some elaborate party before we leave. I'm sure we could use the excuse of buying her and ourselves something suitable to wear as a way to get out of the house. But we need to discuss the schedule of who will guard her throughout the day. Darren, while a formidable foe, is hardly a match for a vampire. Even a weak one. Marcus is guarding Piper now, and we can each easily take turns at night to watch over her, but the daytime will have to be done in shifts."

"I'll take first shift," Rayne volunteered, holding up his hand with a smirk. "She'll probably be in my bed anyway."

"Fucking braggart," Drake muttered under his breath, and Rayne flipped him off with no less of a shit-eating grin. Then

Drake turned to Antoine. "I'll go next. I usually have to get up to piss anyway."

Rayne snickered, earning him another glower from Drake, but he ignored him.

Antoine nodded. "Who's next? I'll take last shift, since technically she should be in my room anyway." This was said to Rayne who stopped laughing to have a stare down with Antoine. Our little brother, who usually backed down from Antoine on all matters, actually held his gaze. Guess he finally found someone worth fighting for.

"I'll go next." Wynn held his hand up lazily, breaking through their stare down. "I do so enjoy watching her eat her meals." Wynn wagged his brows in exaggeration. "Besides, you owe me." He flipped his gaze to Antoine.

Something passed between the two of them, but neither elaborated. "Fine," Antoine clipped, and then turned to me. "Do you wish to go next or closer to evening?"

I lifted a shoulder. "I'm an early riser, so I'm going before you. That still leaves quite a lot of time between lunch and my time though...and what if she wants to go outside?"

Antoine inclined his head. "Marcus has the most stamina of us all and has agreed to bear the brunt of the load."

Drake snorted.

"What?" Antoine snapped, his pale eyes locking on my brother with annoyance. "If you have something to say, say it."

Drake shifted his body weight, and crossed his arms over his chest before leaning back in the seat. "I'm just saying, do we really want Marcus watching over her? He's not exactly a fan."

Antoine's eyes narrowed. "Marcus will do his duty. As all of us will. He has never failed me. Not like some of us." The reminder of my brother's past failure made Drake shrink in his chair before turning his head to the side with a reluctant nod. "Now," Antoine continued with flare, "if there are no other objections, Darren will watch over her during the times she wishes to leave the safety of the house. Unless Valentine or our master has suddenly gained the ability to walk in the sun unhindered, then I believe he will be adequate protection."

We adjourned our meeting. My brother rushed out of the room still in a tizzy about Antoine calling him out. I didn't

162

follow after him. I'd been witness to many of my other half's tantrums, so I didn't need to see this one.

Antoine took his cell phone out and began to dial into it before leaving my room. No doubt he had some business he needed to conduct. It was a good thing overseas hours were so in line with ours, or we wouldn't get any business done at night. Not that Antoine wouldn't have found some other way to fund our lives. He had a knack for those sorts of things.

Rayne and Wynn were all that were left, and they didn't seem in any hurry to leave. Rayne's brows were furrowed and then suddenly he turned to Wynn with wide eyes. "You did what?"

Wynn gave a secretive smile but didn't answer, leaning back against the couch and closing his eyes.

"Don't do that," Rayne growled, shoving at the lounging vampire. "You can't just give me a peek in your head and then shut down like that. Not when it's about her."

Now I was intrigued. Arching a brow, I moved over to the couch near Wynn. "What's he talking about?"

Rayne turned his glare from Wynn to me. "This asshole and Antoine punished

Piper for going off alone. She's already been through enough."

I had to agree. The poor woman might have gotten more than what she had bargained for by being part of our household. In some ways, it might have been better if she had left when she had wanted to before.

"What did you do?"

Wynn cracked one eyes open to give me a lazy smile. "Why don't you ask our fearless leader. It was on his orders."

I huffed. The likelihood that Antoine would give away anything he hadn't already offered freely was slim to none. Thankfully, Rayne gave us a bit of an edge or we'd all be in the dark about a lot of things.

"What'd you see?" I turned to Rayne.

The expression on his face was less appalled and more jealous. It made me all the more curious. "Don't worry about it. She wasn't traumatized or anything."

"Oh, come on," I scoffed impatiently. "You can't just keep that kind of stuff to yourself. This selfish bastard wouldn't talk if the sun itself was asking."

Wynn's lips ticked at my words.

Rayne turned his head away, hiding his eyes, but I could see the redness creeping up his neck and ears. "It wasn't the kind of punishment you need to worry about."

This time I glared accusatorially at Wynn, kicking his shin with my foot. "What'd you do, you pervert?"

A slow grin curled up Wynn's face and he finally opened both eyes to meet my gaze. "I didn't hurt her, if that's what you're thinking. Antoine's the one who turned that gorgeous ass of hers red."

"He spanked her?" I gaped, my eyes widening and my groin tightening at the thought. "She's not a child."

Wynn let out a low chuckle. "No, she is not, based on how turned on she was by it."

"Really?" I mused, shoving my hands into my pockets as I turned this information over in my head. Who would of thought little Piper Billings liked a bit of pain? Good to know.

Still curious to what Wynn had done, I bumped him on the leg again. "Then what'd you do?"

"What I do best." Wynn closed his eyes once more and laced his fingers behind his head.

I glanced over at Rayne and then back to Wynn. "You fucked her? How is that a punishment?"

Rayne chuckled darkly. "No, he didn't even touch her below the neck."

Now I was really confused. What did he do if he didn't screw her brains out? Then it dawned on me. He used his powers on her. But that still didn't sound like a punishment to me. Believe me, if I could make someone come just by touching her skin, I'd be rolling in the ladies. Not that I didn't already get my share with my silver tongue, but still... "I don't get it."

"You and your brother," Rayne sighed and stood, shaking his head while looking at me pitifully. "Bunch of blocks where your brains are, I swear. They wouldn't let her get off. That was her punishment." Rayne stalked out of the room while my face was still frozen in shock.

They wouldn't let her...come? What kind of punishment was that?

"Believe me," Wynn began without prompting, "it was more torture for me than for her. I had to stand there while she moaned and begged for me to get her off, and then just walk away. I had to hide in my room just so I could wank off."

"So, that's why Antoine owes you."

Wynn peeked an eye open. "Not as dumb as he looks."

I rolled my eyes. "Whatever. Don't you have your own room to clog up with your annoying presence?"

Lifting himself from the couch, Wynn trailed his hands down his chest as if he were a stripper on display, but that was just him. So dramatic. "I do, but I am waiting for...ah..." His eyes opened fully, and a devious grin covered his lips. "Sleeping beauty awakens." Then he was gone, leaving me to contemplate how in the world I ended up with such a group of deranged brothers.

Chapter 14
Piper

OPENING MY EYES, I groaned. My hand immediately went to my neck where the pain I'd felt before was now no longer existent. I rushed out of bed and toward the bathroom.

Flipping the light on, I peered into the mirror. I was a scary mess. My blonde hair was a rat's nest and I had bags under my eyes. My skin was so pale that I might as well have been one of the undead. However...I slowly peeled the medical tape away from my neck, revealing the clear skin beneath.

Frowning, I poked gently at the healed flesh. There was only the mark from Antoine's bite. All traces of Valentine had been erased. There was no evidence that he'd ever attacked me. Not any physical evidence, in any case. My skin still crawled as a cold fear rushed up my spine at the thought of seeing him again. I wasn't sure I was going to be able to handle it.

That thought made me hurry to the shower. I turned the water on as hot as it would go and stripped myself of Rayne's clothes. Climbing under the spray, I pushed back the pain of the scalding water as I scrubbed my skin everywhere Valentine had touched me. I scoured until I felt a semblance of clean again, and then wrapped a towel around myself and sank to the bathroom floor mat.

Staring down at the brown, shaggy mat, I thought over what had happened. I couldn't ignore it forever. It wasn't something you could easily push into a drawer and forget about. Valentine had tried to kill me. More than that, he had wanted me afraid.

Part of me blamed myself for antagonizing him. What did I expect a vampire to do? I was stupid to think that

169

I could go against him alone. Still...he was a monster. I couldn't imagine one of my vampires doing the same thing he'd done to me. I shook my head to solidify it. No, they'd never do that to me. No matter how much I angered them.

Sniffling, I pushed myself up off the ground and finished drying. I could have a pity party for myself later. Right now, I had to face them again. I had to face Valentine. My steps wavered at the thought, but I fought through it. Forcing myself back into the bedroom, I dug through my clothing that Darren had graciously put away for me.

I found a pair of pale blue panties and a matching bra, and pulled them on. Grabbing a pair of jeans, I dragged them up my legs, but a knock sounded on the door before I could put my shirt on. Turning to the door, I held the shirt in one hand and prepared to tell them to hold on, but the door handle turned and then opened.

I held the shirt up to my chest as Wynn stepped into the room. "Oh, it's you." I flushed and turned my head to the side as I tucked a stray, wet hair behind my ear. Irritation filled my chest. I hadn't forgotten what he'd done and neither had my body, which still ached from the lack of completion. If I'd had half a mind, I'd have finished myself off in the shower, but my thoughts was elsewhere. "What do you want?"

"Oh, lovely, don't be angry at me." Wynn's provocative voice cooed at me, his footsteps lazy and quiet against the floor. "We all do things we don't want to from time to time."

I snorted and pulled my shirt over my head, not caring if he saw my bra. "Didn't seem like it at the time."

Wynn didn't even pretend not to be looking before his eyes drifted back up my face. "I would never have left you like that had it not been demanded of me. I'm about giving pleasure not pain."

I tossed my head so my hair fell over my shoulder, before grabbing the brush to start working on it. "Well, you can keep your pleasure and your pain. I don't want it."

Wynn sighed and moved closer to me. He moved slowly as if he were afraid to spook me. I didn't blame him, right now, I was spookable. Reaching for the brush, he gestured for me to turn around. I almost didn't let him. I was seconds away from taking that brush and smacking him over the head with it, but then one look into those big, beautiful blue eyes and I saw the pain and regret in them.

I handed the brush over and turned. My breath held as I waited for him to touch me, but he didn't try to take advantage. Wynn smoothed the brush through my hair over and over again in a soothing manner that had me closing my eyes. "You're good at that."

Making an amused sound in his throat, Wynn mused, "I've had centuries of practice. I used to brush my sister's hair."

"You had a sister?"

"Multiple. They were the light of my life...probably why I've spent my whole life trying to find pleasure and give pleasure to women. I never had a good male role model, if you will." Wynn paused, and then continued brushing. "Before I joined Antoine, I'd been a bit of playboy. I seemed to always find my way into some one's bed, male or female, married or not. Probably why our master wanted me. I was pretty and could easily attract new prey for him to devour."

I shuddered. "What changed?" When he didn't answer me, I elaborated. "I mean, why don't you do that anymore? Why did you all leave?"

172

Wynn stopped brushing my hair and set it down on the desk. Taking his place once more, I felt his deft fingers twist and weave my hair. Wynn was so quiet I thought he wouldn't answer me, but then when he finished pulling my newly braided hair over my shoulder, he murmured, "Because of Rayne." Spinning around, I faced him, and I didn't like the sadness on his face. "What about Rayne?"

"Not my story to tell." Giving me a sad smile, Wynn lifted his hand and reached for my face. I hated that I flinched away from him, and when he dropped his hand, I grabbed it, bringing it back to my face. "I'm sorry. For everything. I didn't mean to cause such a mess."

"You didn't, lovely." Wynn cupped my cheek and wrapped his other arm around my waist to draw me closer. "Never think that we regret hiring you or bringing you into our lives, because every single one of us would die for you."

I blinked up at him, astounded by this information.

"Don't look so shocked," he chuckled lightly. "You have quite a way about you, Miss Piper Billings."

"Durand," I corrected him with a grin. "I'm one of you now. Remember?"

"That's right," Wynn agreed, and then gave me a wolfish grin. "Well, I should probably repent, because I don't think any of us think of you as a sister." My face heated.

"I hope not." Then something came to me. "What about Marcus? Surely he doesn't feel the same way."

"You'd be surprised what Marcus thinks and feels. He hides it well, but there's a big marshmallow inside that imposing exterior."

"Pfft. I don't believe it." I shook my head and leaned into Wynn's arms, feeling safe there and less like I might fall apart at any moment.

"Believe it." Wynn rubbed his nose against mine. "He's been guarding your door while you sleep."

"He has?" I tried to move out of his embrace to check, but Wynn held on tight.

"If he hadn't been, I'd have snuck back in here before to finish what I'd started." The husky tone of Wynn's voice caused me to stop in place. My body warmed and I could feel the beginnings of his powers teasing me.

"We can't," I murmured, though I was slickening between my thighs already. "Antoine..."

"Antoine can fuck off." Wynn's hand drifted down to my butt and pressed me firmly against his front, where his hardened cock poked my stomach. "I owe you an orgasm, don't I?" My mouth dried and my breathing quickened. I tilted my head back, my lips ready and waiting for Wynn's kiss. His mouth didn't so much as take mine but coaxed it, like he did everything else. He teased me with his lips, his teeth, and his tongue. I was a puddle of goo in his arms and had to cling to his neck to keep my feet under me. When he lifted me up to wrap my legs around his waist, I moaned, rubbing myself against him. I'd waited for this forever. I cursed myself for taking so long to get to this point with him. I really should have made him my first out of them, but no regrets. I was here with him now.

Wynn walked us over to the bed and lowered me down until my back was on the mattress. I latched on to him, keeping him from moving too far away from me. With a smirk, Wynn released my lips and trailed his mouth down my neck. I

175

moaned as he brushed Antoine's mark, sending new, hot streams of desire through me.

I tried to pull at his clothing, but he caught my hands. "Slow down, pet. We have all the time in the world."

My mind cleared enough to ask, "What about Marcus? He can hear us."

"He's gone off to bed now. As have the rest of our people. Now, do you really want to talk about where everyone is, or do you want to come?" He cupped my hot heat over my pants. I arched into his touch, not wanting him to stop. "I thought so."

Returning his lips to my neck, Wynn made a path over the exposed skin until he got to the neck of my shirt. His hands pushed up the bottom of it until it stopped at my armpits, but he didn't pull it off. Humming in his throat, Wynn caressed my bra-clad breasts, giving special attention to each peak. "I have dreamed of your perfect breasts. Are they as wonderful as I imagined?"

I gasped and pushed myself into his hands as I scrambled to unsnap the bra. I wanted nothing more than to have his hands on my breasts. I was anxious for it.

Then, my stomach growled, the traitorous bastard.

Wynn lifted his head, his eyes crinkling at the sides. "Hungry?"

"No," I lied, trying to bring him back to me. "Not at all. Keep going."

Shaking his head, he moved away from me and offered me a hand. "As much as I regret saying this, I'll have to find out how great your breasts are another time. You need to eat. I should have remembered that."

"No, I don't." I didn't move from the bed, hoping I looked alluring enough to draw him back to me. "I can eat later. I need you now."

Chuckling, Wynn stared down at me with amusement and not as much heat as I wanted. "Yes, you do. You've lost a lot of blood. Antoine's blood can only do so much. Besides..." He leaned down and traced his fingers along the line of my underboob, leaving me quaking beneath his hands. "I don't want you passing out while I ravish you."

"Okay," I squeaked, and jerked my head up and down quickly. "But something quick. Like a sandwich or something. I don't need a lot." I redid my bra and let him lift me up from the bed,

177

while he laughed quietly at my eagerness. I'd have been embarrassed, but I was too damn turned on to care.

Wynn escorted me out of my shared room and into the hallway. My eyes drifted over to a spot to the side of the door and my feet stopped on their own. My heart sped up and any desire I felt dried up like a prune.

That was where Valentine attacked me. Where I almost...I swallowed thickly, my eyes drifting down to the carpet. I didn't see any blood on the runner, but that didn't mean there wasn't any. If there was, my heightened senses were too dull to catch it. Wynn could probably smell it. I almost asked him, but then he wrapped a comforting arm around my shoulders and drew me toward the stairs.

"Come now, pet," he murmured soothingly into my ear. "No need to dwell on it. He'll get his, never you worry."

My head jerked toward Wynn's stoic expression. "What do you mean?"

"Shh, not here. Later." His eyes moved around as if to tell me others were listening.

I nodded reluctantly, but I was impatient to know what they planned on doing to take care of the problem and if I could be part of it.

At the bottom of the stairs, we met with Rayne. He shot an accusatory look at Wynn and announced strangely, "It's my turn."

Wynn lifted a shoulder. "You were busy. I'm taking Piper to get some breakfast. You're free to join us."

I cast a look between the two of them, wondering what the hell they were talking about, but neither of them elaborated. Instead, Rayne huffed and nodded before taking up the empty space on my left. Now, both vampires escorted me through the foyer and down the hallway. We passed the drawing room and library doors, and bypassed the dining room completely to head into the kitchen.

Darren, completely in his element, moved around the kitchen with the other members of the household. Namely, Fauns and a small Asian woman who could have been eighteen or eighty. I couldn't tell one way or the other.

When we stepped into the room, Fauns and the woman stopped what they were doing and dismissed themselves. Darren stayed and went about preparing what smelled like bacon and eggs. I might have said I wasn't hungry, but the moment I smelled the delicious aroma of food, my stomach grumbled once more.

Wynn chuckled beside me and led me to a chair at their breakfast nook. "Not hungry, huh?"

I bumped him with an elbow before taking my seat. I glanced from the table and then to where Darren was, and asked, "Is there—"

Darren turned and brought me a cup of steaming hot coffee before the words even exited my mouth. He sat down the cream and sugar before me as well.

"Thank you," I told him, as I filled my cup with both cream and sugar.

"You're welcome." Darren spun back around, returning to his pans on the stove. Rayne and Wynn took the seats on either side of me, and watched as I drank my coffee. It was a bit unnerving, but I was too happy to have caffeine to care.

"Here." Darren sat a plate in front of me without me asking. It was piled up with meat, eggs, and toast. He also placed a large glass of milk in front of me with a pill. "That's vitamin D and iron. You'll want to take one every day for the next few days, and any time you donate blood afterward."

"Donate," Rayne scoffed, his eyes narrowing. "She didn't donate blood."

Wynn tut-tutted. "Not the time, Rayne." Gritting his teeth, Rayne didn't say another word, but sat there brooding while I shoved food into my mouth.

Darren didn't make a plate for himself and I frowned. "Aren't you going to eat?"

"I already ate." Darren took the last open seat across from me. "That's for you."

Not needing anymore explanation, I continued to eat. Groaning with every bite, I savored the flavors and couldn't believe how good it tasted. Most mornings, I'd usually forgo breakfast and just stick with coffee, but today... Today, it tasted like Nirvana in my mouth.

"Better watch it, love. I'm getting a bit jealous of fried pork."

I paused mid bite to meet Wynn's gaze, and then a quick glanced over at Rayne who had the same kind of intense expression on his face. I flushed and lowered my fork. Picking up my glass of milk, I drank a healthy portion of it before looking across to Darren. He was a safe place to look. Darren at least didn't look like he wanted to be the one eating me.

"So, how do you know so much about what I would need?" I inquired, and then wished I'd swallowed my own tongue. Shaking my head, I smacked my forehead. "Sorry, I blame the blood loss. Obviously, you know what to do. You've been with them long enough you've probably donated your fair share of blood."

Darren's lips twitched. "Not as much as you would think. However, I have had to pick up after the masters for quite some time." He gave a sly glance over to each vampire. "Help keep their leftovers from collapsing on the cab ride home."

I choked on my bite of food, hitting my chest with my fist before reaching for my glass again. When I got the food down, I croaked, "Leftovers?"

"He makes it sound so unsavory." Wynn grimaced, lounging back in his chair. "It wasn't like that at all."

"Wasn't it though?" Rayne countered with a self-satisfied grin. "Did you even know the names of your...donors?"

"Did you?"

Rayne blanched at Wynn's question and then ducked his head. "Most of them. We didn't exactly exchange pleasantries before the donor service."

182

"Precisely," Wynn pointed out with a nod, before turning back to me. "Before the modern age caught up with us, we had to find our meals the old-fashioned way. In bars, on the streets, and even on occasion..." He paused for dramatic effect. "Hospitals."

I hummed, not wanting to think too much on where they got their food supplies or if they'd killed anyone before. I was pretty sure I wouldn't like the answer, and right now I needed them to be the handsome masters from home and not the monster under the bed. I already had one of those. One that I hoped to slay soon.

Chapter 15

Marcus

THIS WAS RIDICULOUS. I was a powerful and mighty vampire. A creature of the night. Not some guard dog. Certainly, not to a puny human woman. I glared at the back of the human maid's head as she walked through the enclosed garden. The flowers were all ones that thrived in the dark at night.

There were prim roses, Casa Blanca Lilies, Queens of the Night, which only bloomed once every year, and my favorite, Chocolate daisies that filled the air with its namesake. There were several others that I didn't know the name of but were equally as exotic. Boris's reach was far and wide. He never skimped on the good stuff.

We'd been walking down the path for a half hour now. Piper had to stop at every single flower to sniff it and give it a good, long look. It was just a fucking flower. How interesting could they be?

"They smell so different than before I was bound," Piper commented, glancing back at me. Her smile wilted at my frowning figure, but I didn't change my stance for her benefit. "You know, you don't have to follow me. I'm perfectly fine with Darren. You can go to bed."

"I have orders," I countered, not giving her room to argue. Except she did anyway.

"Then you can go back to Antoine and tell him to change them. I don't need someone glowering over my shoulder for half the day." She waved me off with a small hand before turning her back to me.

Against my will, my eyes drifted down her small form to hover over her butt. The jeans she wore clung to her curves and would make even the strongest of men fall. I wasn't one of those men.

"I will not." I marched after her with growing irritation. "If you would stay in your room, or any room, I wouldn't have to follow you around."

Piper laughed over her shoulder. I wanted to say the sound of it ground on my nerves, but it was just as lovely as she was. Jesus, fuck.

"Well then, next time I'll just stay in the library. But I need to be outside. I'm human and we need sunlight, even if it's through double paned glass." She frowned up at the ceiling of glass around us. "Besides, walking is good for you. I don't exactly know all the rules of being immortal or whatever, and I'd hate to get fat and be stuck that way forever." She smiled sweetly at me over her shoulder and I felt myself melting.

Forcing a scowl onto my face, I crossed my arms and jerked my head. "Then get walking. You'll need it."

She gaped at me and flipped me off before spinning on her heels and marching away. I grinned at her back, my eyes once more lingering on her backside. I could have told her she needn't worry. Her figure was perfect and would remain that way for the rest of her days.

With heightened senses and quick healing also came a faster metabolism. So, she could eat as much as she wanted and lay around all day, but she'd never get bigger than she was right now. In fact, from the few times I'd seen her eating meals, she could probably eat more.

I strolled along behind her at a close distance without crowding her. I didn't need any more of her intoxicating scent in my nose than I already had now. How Antoine spent time in the same room with her so often baffled me. I didn't consider myself one of the most self-restrained vampires, but I was better than most. However, even I was having a hard time keeping myself from giving into my baser urges.

"Fuck," Piper cried out, holding her hand out in front of her.

Instantly, my fangs ached. The heavy scent of her blood filled the area and I found myself taking a step toward her before I caught myself.

Piper glanced back at me. One look at my face and she stiffened. Her eyes widened and her breathing sped up as she shook her head back and forth. "No, no. Go away." She clutched her bleeding hand to her chest as if that would help the smell.

"Stop panicking, you're making it worse," I instructed, walking toward her.

With wary eyes, Piper let me come toward her but put a hand up before I could get too close. "Stop there. Please."

I stared down at her. Was she dumb? "I need to see it."

"No, you don't," she argued, her lower lip poking out as she cradled her hand closer to her chest. "I'll get a Band-Aid from Darren and it'll be fine. Just stay back."

It finally dawned on me what was wrong. I closed my eyes and focused, taking deep breaths of her scent before opening my eyes once more. "See, I'm not going to go on a blood craze. Now stop being a baby and let me see."

Piper didn't offer me her hand, but she didn't stop me from taking it either. I slowly took her hand in my much larger one and peered down at the cut. It wasn't that deep, barely bleeding.

"What did you cut it on?" I glanced up from her hand to see her point her a finger toward the bush next to her. One of the many night blooming cacti. Of course she'd want to touch that one. "I suggest not touching any others."

"Obviously," she scoffed, glowering at me. "Can I have my hand back now?"

"No," I growled, and then pierced my finger with my thumbnail. Blood welled up at the end of my finger and I started toward her cut.

"Hey now, what do you think you're doing?" Piper tried to pull her hand away, but I held on to it.

"It'll clean it and heal faster."

"So? Doesn't mean I want your blood in me."

I arched a brow. "Is it the fact that it's blood or that it's my blood that's the issue?"

Piper chewed on her lower lip before shoving her hand at me. "Fine. Get it over with. I'm not getting any younger."

I rolled my eyes and reopened the closed cut before tracing the wound on her hand. She hissed and glared at me the whole time, but let me do the job. When I was done, I held her hand and waited for the small cut to close up. Satisfied with her healing, I released her hand and took a step back.

"Wow, I don't think I'll ever get used to that." Piper held her hand up to her face, peering at it like it had sprouted tentacles.

I grunted. "Well, don't get used to it. We shouldn't have to give up our blood to heal you all the time. We might need it for ourselves."

Pursing her lips, Piper placed her hands on her hips and arched a brow. "Well, excuse me for being human and clumsy. I didn't make myself this way. It just happened."

I cocked a brow. "So says the five broken plates, the smashed mirror, the chair in the sitting room, and not to forget the vase during your interview."

Piper turned a pretty shade of red before shooting dagger at me with her eyes. "That's beside the point. All of those had perfectly good reasons behind them and I won't let you bully me. So, you can just go find a stake and sit on it!" She spun on her heel and stomped away, not waiting to see if I'd follow.

I gaped at her, utterly speechless for the first time in my existence. Sure, I wasn't an overly talkative person in the first place, but no one has ever dared talk to me like that. Like she didn't give a damn how big and bad I thought I was, she wasn't going to take any of my shit. I could see how Valentine would want to bite her. I kind of wanted to bite her and then fuck her. Not particularly in that order.

Chapter 16
Piper

FUCKING MEN. FUCKING VAMPIRES. This was stupid. I wasn't five. I could take care of myself. Okay, so I did get almost eaten...twice...and that last one was really close, but still. I didn't need a babysitter everywhere I went. Seriously, I couldn't even go to the bathroom without one of them within hearing distance.

A girl has needs and this girl needed to poop. Badly.

I'd like to keep a little mystery in my newly blossoming sex life, and it was hard to do that when you needed to do unladylike things near said lovers.

"Are you alright in there?" Rayne knocked on the bathroom door after a few minutes of me trying to go to the bathroom.

"I'm fine," I shouted back and then covered my face with my hands. "Could you like...go away?"

Rayne paused and then said, "You know I can't do that, Piper. If Valentine attacks again—"

"He's not going to attack me on the toilet," I growled, picking up a roll of toilet paper and throwing it at the closed door. "I need privacy. Just go out of the bedroom and down the hall. I can't go when you're listening."

"What?" Rayne started and then stopped. "Oh. Oh! Uh, okay. Yeah. I'll just wait outside."

I listened closely until I heard the bedroom door close before I finally went about my business with a sigh of relief. Thank fuck. I was all for not getting killed, but I didn't want to share every aspect of my day with vampires. Being a girl was hard enough, but trying to keep all those habits you kept hidden until you've been together long enough to show your true self, while trying to hide them from someone who could not only hear it but smell it from a different room? Yikes.

When I was finished, I cleaned my hands and made my way out of the bathroom. Moving across my bedroom, I was tempted to hide in the room for the rest of the day just to get some alone time. I couldn't even sleep alone. Though, the last couple of nights I'd hidden out in Rayne's room. Wynn and I had tried to hook back up after breakfast before, but something always got in the way. I had a feeling we weren't going to get another moment alone until we went home.

Home. Now that was something I was surprised to be excited to go back to. Back to cleaning that massive house and running in to each of the vampires I'd come to grow so fond of. Back to Darren critiquing my cleaning methods and hiding the things I've broken. Marcus had named off a few of the things I'd broken, but there were a ton more that I'd gotten rid of before anyone noticed.

One thing I missed a lot was Gretchen's cooking. Darren did well enough in the kitchen, and I wouldn't turn down anything he made, but that woman could cook. Plus, it was nice to have another female in the house. There were plenty of female servants around here and there was even Theresa, but they weren't exactly lining up to talk to me. I think Theresa might prefer to eat me.

"Are you ready to leave?"

I glanced up from where I'd been staring at the floor to see Antoine in the doorway. If he'd knocked, I hadn't heard, but since technically it was his room, I didn't expect him to. I shifted in place, tugging at the hem of the t-shirt dress I'd put on. "I still don't like you buying me clothes. The last time you guys took me shopping, I ended up dressed like a baby prostitute."

Antoine stared up at the ceiling for a moment as if he were praying before walking toward me. He was in one of those well-fitted suits again. I never thought I'd be the kind of girl who loved a man in a suit, but it turns out just seeing him unbutton his cufflinks made my panties wet. He'd also teased me—okay, more like threatened—to tie me up a time or two when I was getting mouthy about being babysat. From the way he played with his tie while saying it told me he had a particular rope in mind.

Not that I was complaining. I'd have been happy to let him tie me down and rock my world. If he actually let me get off. I was still a bit wary of letting him touch me after what happened last time. Antoine seemed to have sensed it and hasn't pushed the matter.

"Our master requires formal wear for all of his parties, and while Darren is a fabulous packer, he didn't pack something suitable for one of our master's events." Antoine walked over to me and lifted a hand to my chin, tipping my face up. "I was wrong to use you to taunt Valentine. I understand my error now. I won't let him touch you ever again."

My mouth fell open. He thought it was his fault? I shook my head, placing a hand on Antoine's jacket-clad arm. Even beneath the fabric, I could feel the muscle there, but I didn't let myself get distracted. "It wasn't you. It wasn't me. It was Valentine. We can't be held accountable for his actions. But I was promised retribution, and if that requires me wearing a poofy dress, then dammit, bring on the frills."

Antoine smiled slightly at that before leaning down to kiss me. I pushed up on my toes to deepen the kiss, but he released me just as quickly. "Come, before I change my mind about tying you to the bed."

My body flushed with the threat, but before I could suggest it, Antoine took me by the arm and led me from the room. Out in the hallway, the others waited for us. Darren had gone to get the limo, but the rest of the household stood in their normal attire at the top of the stairs. Marcus had his eyes on the ground level, while the twins were arguing over something with basketball. Wynn and Rayne both turned to me when I appeared.

I wasn't sure how to handle this situation. Did I kiss them both? Who did I kiss first? What about the others? I wasn't sleeping with them or even close to it, but I liked them...well, not quite Marcus. He was still an asshole.

Thankfully, Rayne got me out of my own conundrum and jerked his head toward the stairs. "Come on, our reservation is at eight. I'm starving."

I rolled my eyes. "You're a vampire. Eating human food isn't going to help."

"It does a bit," Rayne replied, as we turned to head down the stairs. "It takes the edge off at least."

197

"Yeah, plus," Drake added with a grin, "onion rings are the bomb."

I shook my head and giggled. "Nobody says 'the bomb' anymore."

Drake grinned, holding up both hands in with the thumb and forefinger up, and shook them. "Tubular."

Allister smacked him on the back of the head. "They don't say that either. It's badass. Onion rings are badass."

Wynn wrinkled his nose. "No, thank you. The grease. Ugh."

I couldn't stop laughing as the guys continued their discussion on what the best food was. It was such a normal conversation to have. A human conversation. No wonder it took me by surprise when Boris appeared at the bottom of the stairs.

"Ah, good. I caught you before you left." He flashed his long fangs at us. We froze so quickly that you'd think someone had blasted us with nitrogen. None of us had been expecting to see the master of the house. Certainly not now.

"What can we do for you, master?" Antoine answered, shifting me over to take Wynn's arm as he pushed his way down the stairs. "We were just on our way out."

Boris nodded. "Yes, yes. Of course. I won't keep you. I just wanted to have a word with Miss Durand before you left." His bloodred eyes flicked to me and I swallowed thickly.

"Yes?"

Placing a hand on the handrailing of the stairs, he put on an expression of sympathy that didn't reach his eyes. "I wanted to apologize for my child's actions. Valentine can let his baser urges get the better of him when it comes to pretty women. I hope you don't hold his actions against me?" He placed his hand on his chest, and if he had them, he'd have fluttered his eyelashes at me.

My heart rate ratcheted up a level and I had to remind myself that I was safe. I was surrounded by not one, but all six of my vampires. He couldn't touch me. Valentine wasn't even here. Taking a deep breath, I forced a smile onto my lips. "Of course not. A parent cannot be blamed for the actions of their children."

Boris clasped both hands together and smiled in return. "I'm so happy you agree. Have no fear, I have sent Valentine away to fetch some of our guests for the party on Friday, so you shouldn't have to worry about him popping up unexpectedly." His

199

eyes moved to the vampires around me. "And I can see you have plenty of guardians to protect you when he does return. I hope they, too, can find it in their hearts to forgive their brother for his lapse in judgment."

The others inclined their heads, but it was clear that none of them meant it. They knew what Boris's words were and they weren't a gracious offer of peace. They were a warning to leave it alone or else. Too bad none of us planned on following it.

"Good." Boris turned toward the door, waving a hand at it before bowing slightly. "Then have a lovely evening."

With permission to move, we slowly made our way down the stairs and out the door with Wynn and I taking up the rear. Before I finished getting out the doorway, Boris called out to me.

"Yes?" I twisted around to face him.

With smile that could have been called calculating, Boris gestured to me. "Do find something in red, my dear. I hear you look lovely in that color."

It was a good thing that Wynn had me by the arm or I'd have fallen over dead right there. Thankfully, Boris didn't expect me to reply and allowed Wynn to drag me out of the house and into the evening air.

Once we were in the car, I wrapped my arms around myself and rocked. "I can't breathe. I can't..." I gasped in lungfuls of air, but never seemed to get enough in. I shouldn't have come here. I should never have come here. God, fucking, fuck. Fuck, fuck.

"Piper!" Rayne yelled in my face, his hands on either shoulder. My eyes finally cleared to allow me to see him and I croaked out a rasping breath. "Breathe, Piper. You have to calm down and breathe."

"You got to show her, you dumbass. Here." Drake shoved Rayne aside and took his place. My vision was starting to dim, and I knew I was going to pass out if I didn't get enough air. Drake placed his hands on either side of my face and I could feel his powers of persuasion against my skin. "Breathe in, breathe out. In and out. That's it, girl. In and out." He repeated the process until I was able to drop my arms and breath on my own. "Better?"

I nodded. "Yes, thank you."

"No problem." Drake winked before moving back to his seat on the opposite side of the limo against the driver's seat. Allister sat next to him, worry etched on his face. In fact, everyone, including Marcus, had a similar expression. Offering a weak smile, I shifted toward them. "I'm fine now. Really."

"Are you sure?" Rayne moved from his seat to kneel in front of me again. "Because we can go back and stake that bastard right now." He gestured over his shoulder. I thought he was kidding. I hoped he was kidding.

I shook my head. "No, it's okay. Don't go getting killed on my account. We still have to get rid of Valentine first." The words no sooner came out of my mouth when I realized that we might not be alone. My hand jumped to my mouth and I stared at the divider.

"Don't worry, it's just Darren," Rayne answered the question I hadn't asked, then immediately added on, "Sorry, habit."

I ruffled his hair and smiled until he came close to me, then I grabbed a handful of hair and pulled until his neck bent sideways. "It's fine if I'm in danger. But keep getting into my thoughts and you're going to hear something you won't like."

202

"Ah, ah, ah. Geez, fine. I said I was sorry." I released him and Rayne grunted. "You might like a bit of pain, but I'm not into that kind of stuff."

My face went beet red and my eyes darted to Antoine and Wynn. "So, you're just telling everyone now? What happened to privacy?"

Antoine shrugged. "Do not point fingers at me until you are prepared to have them bitten."

I shifted my gaze to Wynn who didn't even bother to have the decency to be ashamed. "What can I say? He beat it out of me."

"No, I didn't," Rayne argued, getting up and banging his head on the ceiling. "Fuck." Rubbing his head, he glared at Wynn. "You thought it, very loudly while touching me. I can't keep everything out."

I pursed my lips and sighed, shaking my head. "This is going to keep happening, isn't it? I guess I shouldn't be surprised. That's what I get for dating vampires who live together."

"Dating, huh?" Wynn gave a sly grin. "I wasn't aware we had reached that point in our relationship."

I sank down in the seat and chewed on my lower lip. "Well, I...uh...I just..."

"He's fucking with you, Piper." Allister shoved Wynn's shoulder. "Give the girl a break. She just relearned to breathe, she doesn't need you giving her another heart attack."

Thankful for Allister's involvement, it was completely out of left field when Drake asked, "So, when do I get a turn?"

"What?" I choked out, my eyes bugging from my head. "What do you mean, when do you get a turn?"

Drake leaned forward, propping his elbows on his knees and grinned. "You know. To take you out. Allister and I would both like to have the chance to woo you. You still call it that now, don't you?"

I nodded, my face even redder than before. "Yes."

"Good. Then we want a turn."

I glanced between the two of them, and God help me, but the first thing that came to mind was both of them *wooing* me at the same time. Rayne snickered and I kicked his shin from my seat.

"Ow!" Rayne rubbed his leg. "What'd I do?"

I narrowed my eyes at him. "You know."

Thankfully, I didn't have to answer the twins' question right then because the limo stopped. Darren came around and opened the door. "We're here."

I scrambled to get out first. "Thank God. I need a drink."

Chapter 17
Rayne

THE WHOLE HOUSEHOLD HADN'T gone to dinner in ages. Certainly not with someone like Piper. A part of me wanted nothing more than to have her to myself, while the other part didn't want to be selfish. My brothers hadn't had the greatest luck with finding love and it seemed that Piper was made for us. She was certainly made for me.

"How many?" the hostess asked, eyeballing our group with obvious lust in her eyes and on her mind. When her eyes moved to Piper, her smile dipped. *Lucky whore.*

"We have a reservation." Antoine stepped in. "Durand. Party of eight."

The hostess looked down at her podium, and then with a large smile said, "Just give us one moment, I'll check and see if your table is ready."

"Eight?" Piper questioned, looking around and then spotting Darren. "Oh, right."

"Did you think we'd make poor Darren wait out in the car?" Drake grinned, throwing an arm over her shoulders. "He's been with us longer than you have. Though, I never wanted to fuck him."

"Draconius," Antoine chastised with a shake of his head. "Children. After all these years, you're still children." Piper blushed hard at the enormous twin. "Uh, no. Just haven't seen him out of the house...like, ever."

Darren snorted before stopping next to Piper. "Just because you do not see me leave the house does not mean I do not have a life. I play chess with a very nice group of men down at the park every Saturday."

Beaming over at Darren, Piper waved a finger in his face. "Would that happen to be the old men's club I see out there? You wouldn't be playing with them, would you?"

With a frown, Darren adjusted his gloves and then his jacket. "I'll have you know that I am three times their age and they are far more stimulating than this lot. Well, some of them." Antoine and Darren exchanged a look and a flash of something I never wanted to see hit my head.

"Oh, my god. I'm scarred for life." I covered my eyes and groaned. "Please, no thinking about naked fun time with my brother around me."

The others laughed at me before going on to talk about what they planned on eating when we were seated. The hostess thankfully reappeared a few minutes later and we were escorted to our table. Walking through the restaurant, I scanned the crowd. For a Wednesday night the place was pretty busy. Almost every table was filled with people, and the thoughts pouring in from around me made me wince and want to cover my ears.

A small hand slipped into mine, giving it a squeeze. I glanced down at Piper's concerned face.

"Are you okay?" she asked, raising her voice over the crowd.

I leaned down next to her ear and said, "You don't have to raise your voice, I can hear you even over this deafening nonsense." I squeezed her hand in return and had the urge to kiss her, so I did. Pecking her on the lips, I was happy to feel her trying to linger in the kiss, but it wasn't the time or place to be making out so openly.

Pulling back, Piper stared at me hotly and licked her lips. *When we get home, I'm going to rip your clothes off.*

Distracted by her words, I didn't see the guy pushing his chair out and my foot caught on the edge of it, sending me careening onto the floor. The area quieted for a second, and Piper rushed to my side, half laughing and half concerned.

"Oh, my god. Are you alright?" she inquired through her laughter. "You really should watch where you're going."

I shot her a warning look before reaching out and grabbing her hand, and pulling her to my chest on the floor, tickling her sides. "I'll show you, watch where I'm going indeed. If someone wouldn't have been trying to distract me."

209

Piper giggled and fought against me, pushing at my chest. "Stop, stop. I'm sorry. Just stop tickling me."

A throat cleared next to us, followed by a silent demand of, *Rayne,* from Antoine, finally made me stop. I sighed and stood up before helping Piper off the ground. I brushed myself off and tried to help clean Piper up but she batted my hands away with a smirk.

The restaurant guests were still staring at us. I held my hands up and shifted around. "Sorry, my bad. Nothing to see here." Thankfully, the silly humans returned to their meals and we were brought to our table.

Sitting at a circular table with Piper at my side and the others lined around the rest of it, our waiter greeted us. With a bright smile and a good boy attitude that poured into his demeanor, he announced, "Hello, I'm Phillip and I'll be serving you today. What can I get you started with?" Everything would have been fine had Phillip not been staring at Piper the entire time he was talking, ignoring the seven other men around her. *Look at that rack. God, what I would do to those if I had some butter.*

Before I knew it, a low growl was coming out of my throat and Phillip startled, his eyes going wide and more importantly, getting off of Piper. Drake, who sat next to me, nudge me with his elbow, making me cough. I picked up my water and took a drink before turning my eyes back to Phillip. "Sorry, something was in my throat."

Giving a nervous chuckle, Phillip nodded while holding his order pad close to him. "Can I get you all something to drink?" He looked around the table and frowned. In his head, he wondered if we were some kind of boy band or modeling group. Then his eyes landed on Piper again. *Is she fucking them?*

"Yes, yes she is," I answered out loud, freaking Phillip out.

Fuck, did I say that out loud? "Oh, my god, I'm sorry. I don't know why I said that. Please don't tell my manager," Phillip rushed to apologize, thinking that he had indeed said it out loud, because who would believe I could read his mind?

Smirking, I threw my arm over Piper's shoulder and shrugged. "It's cool. Just don't let it happen again. I want a beer. What about you, baby?" I turned my eyes to Piper, giving her my best smolder.

Flushing under my attention and quite confused, she stuttered out, "Uh, I'll have a water and a glass of the rosé."

Phillip scrambled to write down our orders and then everyone else's. When he left, Piper flicked my nose, making me flinch. "What was that for?"

Pursing her lips, Piper scowled. "You know what. Keep out of people's heads. You about gave that poor waiter a heart attack."

"Yeah," Drake added in with a grin. "Or at least let the rest of us in on the fun. It's like being invited to a party but not being allowed to dance."

"You like to dance?" Piper leaned over me to ask, putting her boobs right against my chest. "I love to dance."

"You do, huh?" Drake purred, leaning on his elbow so he was practically giving me a lap dance right there. "I'll have to take you some time. My brother and I are the best dancers."

Wynn made a rude sound. "If you call grinding your pelvis against a lady dancing."

Drake moved back to his seat so he could glare at Wynn a few chairs down. "I do. The ladies love it." He shot Piper a wink.

"In my day, a man kept a foot between him and his dance partner at all times," Wynn explained with a lazy grin. "It was all about the buildup. The teasing of it all."

Piper's scent spiked next to me.

I placed my hand on her thigh, happy she had chosen to wear a dress tonight. She froze under my touch, but then relaxed as I played my fingers along her inner thigh.

Clearing her throat, Piper put her elbow on the table and fiddled with her dangling earrings, keeping her eyes off of me. "Oh, really? That sounds like fun. What about you Antoine? What was dancing like when you were hu—" The waiter returned with our drinks and Piper rushed to change her words. "When you were a humanitarian." She let out a nervous giggle. "You know, those big parties you threw for...uh...the donors?"

I chuckled under my breath at her fumble, squeezing her knee beneath the table. Piper gave me a chastising glare before thanking Phillip for her drink. When the waiter finished passing out our drinks, we ordered our food and then waited for Phillip to leave once more.

Antoine lifted his red wine to his lips and took a long sip before saying, "Dancing was more of an art and less of a way to find one's mating partner." His eyes locked on to Drake and Wynn. "The ability to move your body in sync with the music as well as your dance partner was the goal. Not who could get away with fucking on the dance floor."

Piper's scent spiked again. Her thighs clenched together beneath my hand. So she likes it when prim and proper Antoine says fuck, huh? I held back a grin at my discovery.

"So, what else?" Piper glanced around the table. "I know you guys all came from Boris, right? I mean, he made you all? Sired? Is that the right word?"

"Yes," Antoine answered, and then tilted his head to the side. "And no. Our master changed all of us except for Rayne, who I changed but he does not have any pull over us. You see, while we might have a multitude of powers, our master—Boris—doesn't have any powers over the ordinary."

Piper's nose scrunched up in a cute manner. "Why not? I would think you'd have to be pretty powerful to make all of you." She gestured around the table.

"Not so," Wynn continued, taking over for Antoine. "A child doesn't inherit a parent's talent, nor does the parent have all of the child's abilities. It's the same basic concept. Except in this one, we're vampires." Wynn flashed her a fang toothed grin.

Call me selfish, but I wanted Piper's attention back on me and not on my brothers. It was the excuse I used when I slid my hand between Piper's thighs and inched my way up her panties. Keeping my eyes forward, I listened with a growing smirk to the thoughts running through Piper's head.

Rayne. What are you doing? Out loud, Piper cleared her throat and took a long drink of her wine. "And what about the house sigil? You all have it tattooed? Even you, Darren?"

I stroked across the front of her panties, the fabric becoming wet, and she opened her legs wider for me.

Darren—none the wiser of what was happening beneath the table—met Piper's gaze. "No, only the masters of the house wear the sigil."

"Why?" Piper's word caught at the end as I circled her clit. By now, Drake and

215

Marcus were glancing this way, fully aware of what was going on.

Antoine answered for Darren. "Because to be branded by one of the masters with the house sigil is to mark you as our property. I have far too much respect for Darren to do such a thing."

"Regardless of my opinion," Darren interjected. It was clear to everyone that Darren would have happily wore our sigil, but what he saw the sigil as wasn't the same thing as Antoine did. I didn't blame him one bit. Antoine didn't see Darren as his property and the other vampires wouldn't allow Darren to think for himself. They'd defer everything to Antoine, as if Darren was a slave of sorts. Not someone anyone who cared for someone would do to another person.

I quickened my pace over Piper's clit and watched as the entire tables' noses flared while Piper stifled a moan.

"Are you alright, lovely?" Wynn asked, amusement pulling at his lips. "Are you going to be sick?"

Gasping, she smacked the table with her hand and shook her head. "No, I'm...I'm alright. Just hungry." She gave a weak smile that wasn't fooling anyone.

"You know," Allister turned to Antoine, "I was thinking of *coming* to the party a bit late tomorrow. What do you think? When will you be *coming*, Piper?"

Still not in on the joke, Piper chewed on her lip and croaked out, "Uh, I don't know. Whenever Antoine wants me to come."

I grinned broadly, meeting Antoine's eyes as I flicked my finger against her clit. "Yes, Antoine. When should Piper come?"

Picking up his wine glass, Antoine watched Piper's face while he took a drink. Then pushing some power behind his voice, he stated, "Now."

Piper shuddered beneath my hand, letting out a tiny cry that startled dear Phillip who made the terrible timing of showing up then. I removed my hand and smiled up at the waiter. "She's fine. Just a bit lightheaded from the wine is all."

"Okay," Phillip drawled as Piper gathered her bearings. "Your food will be out in just a moment. Does anyone need a refill?"

I glanced over at Piper, bumping her with my shoulder. "What do you think, baby? Do you want some more?"

Piper looked confused for a second and then glanced around the table before narrowing her eyes on me. "No. I'm good."

"Are you sure?" Phillip asked again, not seeming to want to leave the table.

"You heard the woman," Drake replied with a chuckle. "She's good."

"Okay, then." Phillip turned on his heel and left.

The moment he was gone, Piper stood up and scowled. "You're a bunch of assholes," she growled, before storming off toward the bathroom.

The table chuckled, even Marcus, the unfeeling robot, let out a snicker.

"So, now that we're out of the house. How are going to get rid of Valentine?" Drake leaned forward on the table, his eyes rounding the chairs. "I say we jump him in a dark alley and cut his head off. Then we can cut the other limbs off. Burn them, and then dump them out of the plane home."

"Or..." His brother drew out with a what the fuck look on his face. "We could do something a little less serial killer and just stake him."

Drake huffed and crossed his arms. "Fine. Take all the fun out of it."

"The main thing to focus on is how to do it without getting caught," I pointed out with a nod. "Valentine has a lot of enemies. Maybe we can make it look like one of them did it."

"I like that idea." Wynn shifted in his chair, stroking his chin. "Perhaps at the party? There will be plenty of people to put the blame on there. Plus, our master will think all is forgiven and forgotten."

I gritted my teeth, my fingers curling tightly into fists. "No way would I ever forgive or forget what that bastard did. He deserves what's coming to him."

"Agreed." Antoine inclined his head and then turned to Marcus. "Is it possible?"

Marcus was quiet for a moment. I even tried to peek into his head but he, out of all of us, was the one with the best mental defenses. Then after a long pause, he nodded his head so slightly you would have missed it had you not been looking. "Yes. I believe so."

"So, we get Valentine away from the crowd during the party and do the deed then. How will we dispose of the body?" Allister questioned, dragging a hand through his short hair. "It's going to be hard with all those people there."

Marcus smirked. "Not that hard."

"What about Piper?" I reminded everyone with a pointed look. "She's going to need protection from our master and whoever else he brings to this thing. We don't have that many friends either."

"We can't all go when it happens." Drake shrugged. "I volunteer to rip Valentine's throat out."

"No, I want to do it," I argued with a growl. "If anyone has the right to rip that guy apart, it's me."

Drake laughed, throwing his head back. "You? You couldn't kill Darren, let alone Valentine. Let someone with experience and muscle behind their punches do it."

"Neither of you will be there," Antoine commanded, making us quieten. "Two people. Only two is all that is needed to take down Valentine. Wynn and I will do it." I groaned with the others, annoyed at missing my chance for blood. "The rest of you need to keep our master distracted and Piper safe. We don't need all of us under the ax if it all blows up in our faces."

"Fine," I grumbled. "But I get to stay with Piper. Boris gives me the creeps." I shuddered and the others gave me a sympathetic look. I didn't like to talk

220

about it much, because I didn't want to dwell on the past, but Antoine saved me. Not just by changing me, but by stepping in to keep Boris's attention off of me. While Valentine had a thing for small blond women, Boris liked boys. Preferably as young as possible. And when he couldn't find one to fit his needs, he would turn to his household. He'd turn to me.

My dark thoughts were interrupted by the waiter bringing out our food and then Piper showed back up. This time when she sat down, she scooched her chair closer to Marcus and crossed her legs.

"So, what's everyone talking about? When do we kill Valentine?"

Chapter 18
Piper

IT WAS JUST SO gorgeous. I didn't know how I'd ever take it off the hanger. All that fabric, the lace and silk combination. I just...I grinned, chewing on my lower lip.

I didn't know how I let the guys talk me into this. How was I even going to get it on by myself? There was just so much to it. I had a hard enough time getting into the lingerie they'd bought for me to wear underneath. I pulled up the top of my red, thigh-high hose, and unclipped and reclipped the garter belt. I'd never worn this much for a man, let alone just to wear a dress. I had a feeling the guys liked to use me as a dress up doll. This was their excuse to get me into whatever they wanted me to wear.

Pushing up my tits in the strapless, matching corset, I smirked. If my normal, boring underwear got them all riled up, I couldn't wait to see what this outfit did to them. For a moment, I stared at my dress while daydreaming over who might be disrobing me tonight. A shiver of pleasure ran through me and I giggled.

Stepping into my high heels, I leaned down to buckle them. While my world was upside down, the bedroom door opened. I tilted my head to the side, shoving my hair out of my face.

"Well, this is a view I could get used to." Wynn's eyes devoured my form and I quickly stood up. All the blood rushed to my head and I stumbled. Wynn appeared at my side, and he wrapped his arm around my waist, pulling me against his chest. "Woah, there."

I gasped and held on to his arms. "Thanks. I don't wear heels much."

"Uh-huh," Wynn muttered, his eyes focused on the cleavage seconds away from popping out of my corset.

I flushed and smacked him on the arm. "My eyes are up here, you know?"

Wynn's hand stroked up and down my back before lifting his gaze to mine. "I have a new rule in the house."

"What?"

"You must always clean the house in this." He leaned away from me so he could really take in my lingerie. "Could you turn around, and maybe reach for something on a high shelf? Maybe call me master?"

I shoved him and giggled. "No. Geez. I couldn't get anything clean dressed like this. Plus, my feet would be killing me after a few minutes."

Wynn snorted. "You wouldn't be on your feet for long."

Shaking my head, I turned toward the dress. "While you're here, think you could give me a hand?"

"Oh, lovely. I have been waiting for you to ask me that." Before I could figure out what Wynn meant, I was jerked off my feet and in his arms once more. Cupping my cheeks, Wynn brushed his nose against mine, before nipping my lips with his teeth. I reached up and curled my fingers into the dark curls around his face, tugging him closer.

"So impatient," Wynn murmured, licking his lips so that his tongue trailed along mine. He flicked it against the crease of my mouth, and I opened beneath him. The wet muscle danced in my mouth, rubbing and rolling against mine. Fingers found the skin between my thigh highs and garters. Lifting my leg up and around his hip, Wynn ground his hardness against the junction of my thighs.

Gasping, I pulled back from Wynn's mouth and thrust my hips closer. "Wynn, I have to get ready. We have the party..." I tried to open my eyes and find the clock in the room, but gave up when Wynn began kissing down the line of my neck. "Uh, no, come on. Oh, fuck it."

Wynn growled his approval and lifted my other leg. I squealed as he walked us over to Antoine's bed and dropped me onto it.

I bounced slightly, but grinned up at him. Touching my tongue to my teeth, I played with the buttons of Wynn's dark blue shirt, dipping my fingers beneath it. "This is naughty. Doing it on someone else's bed."

Wynn arched a brow. "If you think this is naughty, oh, I could tell you some stories."

I wrapped my legs around his waist and pulled him closer. "Not the time." Wynn slid his fingers under the front laces of my corset, and started to pull at it. I grabbed his hand and shook my head. "No, no way. It took an hour to get this thing on. You can see my boobs another time. Just fuck me like I always dreamed you would."

Arching a brow at me, he smirked. "Oh, love. You don't have to tell me twice." Wynn reached beneath the garters and pulled my underwear down with a low groan. "God, you smell good."

I lifted my hips and parted my thighs for him. All of my employer-worker fantasies were coming true. I'd been thinking of this day since I first saw Wynn in that drawing room, ever since he wrapped my hand up after I broke that vase. I couldn't count the number of times I'd touched myself thinking about this moment.

Sure, it wasn't how I imagined it, but I wouldn't have it any other way.

Wynn's longer fingers sought out my center, stroking and teasing me until I was gasping for more. I bucked against his hand, and then suddenly it was like he was touching somewhere deep inside of me that I'd never even touched myself.

"What? What is that?" I gasped, my eyes rolling into the back of my head as my spine arched off the bed.

Wynn kissed my thigh. "Just my regular brand of vampire."

That was when I realized he was using his powers on me. Groaning, I grabbed his shoulder, digging my nails into his flesh. "That's...that's cheating."

"Want me to stop?"

"Fuck no," I screeched, as fireworks exploded behind my eyes. Before I had a chance to catch my breath, Wynn slid between my thighs, and then I was relearning how to breathe all over again. If I thought his powers were overwhelming before, nothing compared to having him inside of me. Every inch of me was on fire and I couldn't get enough. I didn't even care about what awaited us downstairs or even about Valentine. All I knew was Wynn. Wynn. Wynn.

"Oh, fuck," I gasped into his mouth as I found my release again. Wynn slowed, pumping into me a few more times before groaning against me.

Lifting his head, Wynn brushed his lips against my lips, my cheeks, and then my forehead. "Whatever happens tonight, I want you to remember this moment. Right here. Because I will. For the rest of my existence and after."

I frowned at Wynn for a moment and then laughed. "What are you going on about? What's happening tonight?"

Wynn withdrew from me and shook his head with a lopsided grin. "Nothing. Forget it. I'm getting maudlin is all. Let's get you dressed before Darren gets in here and starts griping about me messing up his artwork."

I sat up, still frowning. I wasn't sure if I believed him. Something was going on. Not anything good, I was sure.

Slipping off the bed, I pulled my panties back on and shuffled over to the bathroom to check my hair and makeup. Darren really was a master at doing hair. I never had this much body or curl to my hair in my life. Turning back to the bedroom, I walked over to the dress that I was still surprised I was going to get to wear.

Lifting the dress off the hanger, I held it out to Wynn. He opened the back for me to step into the red, tutu lace evening gown. The bottom was so long that it trailed behind me when I walked. I pulled the sheer, long-sleeved lace sleeves up and turned. Wynn's fingers caressed my skin as he buttoned up the back. I swept my hair over my shoulder, exposing my neck so he could get the rest of the buttons. When he was done, Wynn leaned down and kissed the side of my neck, nipping at it and making me gasp.

"You look beautiful," Wynn murmured into my ear, his hands grasping my hips. "Keep your wits about you tonight. There will be many games afoot and none of them you want to lose."

"I will." I watched him in the mirror, trying to read his face, but he had a good poker face going on. I'd have to pick an easier target. Maybe Rayne. He was easy to twist around my finger.

The door to the bedroom opened and in came the very person I wanted to see. Rayne was dressed in a suit and bow tie. His red hair was slicked back and he had a bashful look on his face. "Piper, wow. You look...great. Really, wow."

I turned around and smiled. "You do too. I don't think I've ever seen you so cleaned up."

Scratching his ear, Rayne ducked his head. "Yeah, well, Antoine isn't that fond of elaborate parties like our master is. Thank fuck." His eyes moved to Wynn who had a smug expression on his face. Rayne's eyes widened and then sniffed the air. "Did you two just..." His eyes trailed over to the bed. "Antoine is going to be pissed when he finds out you fucked on his bed."

I crossed my arms over my chest. "He'll only know if you tell him."

Wynn snorted, and then Rayne laughed and said, "Oh, he'll know without us saying anything."

Spinning around to Wynn, I smacked him on the chest. "You did this on purpose, didn't you? You just wanted to get at Antoine."

Wynn wrapped his arms around my waist, but I didn't lean into his embrace, instead pouting my lower lip. "Lovely, it never even crossed my mind. I was too consumed by your beauty and..." His hands slid down my hips, cupping my butt through my dress. "Feminine wiles."

I dropped my arms and peered up at him. "Really?"

Rayne scoffed. "Don't listen to him. I can see in his head. He might have been thinking about you, but he was also thinking about Antoine's face when he came in here later."

Wynn growled at Rayne who smirked. "Someday, you're going to get into the wrong person's head and then end up in the ground."

I pushed out of Wynn's arm and shook my head. "Antoine's right. You might be old as dirt, but you still act like immature boys." I moved over to the desk and picked up the earrings I was going to wear tonight. Poking one through the hole while looking in the mirror, I scolded over my shoulder, "Really, come on. You don't see me trying to rub you in each other's faces, do you?"

"That's because you're the one getting all the benefits," Rayne pointed out with a huff. "We have to take turns. While you get your pick."

I arched a brow and twisted my other earring around in my hand. "Do you think I planned this? I was only looking for a job. Not a hook up. Especially not with more than one guy. My past self would be appalled at me. Hell, my own mother would blow a gasket if she ever knew." I paused, thinking as I slid the other earring home. "Well, if she remembered anyway. I'm sure you'd wipe that right from her memory too. In any case, I care about you all the same. I haven't played favorites...well, not much," I added, when Wynn arched a brow at me. "I won't now. So, you can stop having pissing contests, because I'm with you all. Not just one or the other. And since we kind of have forever...I don't plan on picking just one of you. Are you okay with that?"

Wynn and Rayne stared each other down before turning to me.

"I'm agreeable to it," Wynn stated, walking over to me and lifting my hand up to kiss it. "As long as you make room for me in your heart and in your bed, I'll stop."

"Good." I smiled at him softly and then turned to Rayne. "Well?"

Rayne sauntered over to me, but didn't take my hand like Wynn had. He jerked me against him and captured my mouth with his, kissing me until my toes curled and my knees weakened. Rayne released me with a smirk. "Yeah, I'm good with it." Clearing my throat, I touched up the corners of my lipstick. "Well, since that's settled, I say let's get this party started."

Rayne chuckled and shook his head, taking my arm in his. "You say that now, but in about ten minutes you're going to wish you were back in here arguing with us."

"Why?" My brows rose in confusion.

Wynn took my other arm and looped it through his, patting my hand. "You'll see. If nothing else, our master is a master of the dramatics and overindulgence."

Chapter 19

Antoine

WHEN WE LIVED HERE before, I hated these parties. Now that I didn't live here, I loathed them.

I wanted nothing more than to go home and return to my normal routine. I couldn't believe I was thinking this, but I'd rather be doing paperwork. God, I was in vampire hell.

Our master always had a thing for elaborate gestures that made a statement, and usually those statements were, 'look how much money I have,' or 'look how important I am.' Look at my large, custom-made ballroom with its glass chandeliers and hand painted ceilings of naked babies. There should be a law against vampires having innocent little babies naked on their ceilings. They were angels, which only made it worse.

"Why the sour puss, Antoine?" My master stepped up beside me, dressed in one of his extravagant suits—purple and blue everywhere. I was lucky he wasn't wearing a top hat. Oh, wait, there it was. Setting his hat on his head, my master flashed me a fanged grin. "It's a party. You should be having fun. I see your lovely lady is."

My eyes followed his to where Piper was dancing with the twins. They were taking turns spinning her around the dance floor, causing Piper to giggle and hold her head when she got dizzy. I was happy she was able to have some fun tonight. I only wished it were under different circumstances. Perhaps, I'd have to have more parties at home. I loved to see her smile that way and my chest was pulsating with the emotions coming from her.

"Yes, well, I'm just a bit peckish is all," I drawled, keeping my eyes on Piper and my brothers. I discreetly also kept an eye on the vampires around the room. Many of them I had lived here in the mansion with for centuries. Rarely did a vampire leave this house would without their souls ripped to shreds like Valentine, and now, they were watching Piper like she was the hot new item on the menu.

"Well..." My master clapped me on the shoulder and steered me away from the dance floor. "Why don't you come over here and taste some of the fine options we have for this evening." I forced back a grimace as he ushered me over to the buffet table. In various stages of undress, the 'donors'—which were more often than not just charmed—sat along the edge of the buffet table. Many of them had bites lining their necks and arms, since most of the vampires here were too selfish and inconsiderate to heal them before leaving them.

"Here you are, take your pick." My master swept his hand down the line and then pointed at a young gentleman who was barely eighteen. "You must try this one. It's delicious."

The way he talked about humans like they were only food and not intelligent beings sickened me. It made me wonder how I ever thought this man could be a safe haven for anyone. I should never have brought Piper here.

To the right of me, a long blonde-haired woman with soft brown eyes cried out. A vampire knelt between her thighs, taking blood from the femoral artery. The woman let out a small whimper before collapsing on the table, her eyes wide and empty. The familiar, strawberry blond head stood up from the ground, licking his lips.

Turning to me, he gave me a wolfish grin. "Well, I guess she's done. I didn't mean to drain her dry but..." He trailed off, his eyes sliding toward Piper on the dance floor. "She was just so damn good."

My fingers curled into tight fists and I couldn't help myself from taking a step toward him. Valentine grinned as if begging me to come at him.

Our master stepped between us with a chuckle. "Now, now, boys. This is a party, no fighting. And Valentine..." He tut-tutted, patting him on the chest. "Bad form. Save some for the rest of us."

"My apologies, master." Valentine bowed slightly to him, before lifting his gaze to me and smirking. "I'll be sure to share in the future."

"That's my boy, now go have some fun." Our master chuckled and then shifted to me. "I'm going to see if I can get a bit more out of that one over there, but feel free to taste any of them, just don't get too carried away. Disposing of bodies in the modern age is a pain in the ass." He winked and chuckled before walking back toward the young man.

I glanced down the line of donors and my appetite disappeared. How was I ever like this? Was I just a completely deranged animal?

A large shadow fell over me and without looking, I asked, "Are we prepared?"

"Everything is ready," Marcus answered, not bothering to lower his voice. In a room full of vampires, it was hard to keep a secret. We'd perfected the art of speaking in code. We had to in this house or we wouldn't have survived.

"Very well, and does she suspect?" I turned to face the dance floor once more, where Piper slow danced with Wynn. I had hoped to get a dance in with her myself, but it would have to wait until after. There was too much at stake tonight. Personal needs would be put on the back burner.

"Not that I'm aware."

"Rayne," I said in a normal tone, gaining the youngest member of my household's attention from across the room. In a moments time, he appeared next to me. *Does Piper suspect anything? I don't want her involved in this.*

Rayne stared at the lovely blonde for a moment, and then replied, "She knows something is going on but not what. Though, I'm sure she has guessed that as well. Our girl isn't dumb."

"No," I murmured, taking a glass of warmed blood off a passing tray. "She's not." I drained the glass. I would need all my strength for this, and I didn't want to give Valentine the upper hand by starving myself to save my own morals.

We watched Piper dance in silence. This would be a big night for us all. If things go wrong... *Get Piper and the others out of here if something happens. Do you understand me, Rayne?*

Rayne nodded. "Of course. I won't fail you." He paused, and stared hard at the dance floor. "I won't fail her."

I know you won't. My eyes found Valentine in the crowd. He chitchatted with a few of the local vampires who had shown up to play, before making his way to the terrace. Valentine had one weakness, one thing that still kept him human.

239

Smoking.

It was a habit he picked up in life and had carried over into his undeath. He was addicted to it. Like clockwork, he would go out to smoke every two hours regardless of what he was doing. He'd tried to smoke inside, but our master hated the smell and insisted he go outside. We planned on using that weakness against him.

"It's time." I adjusted my tie and slipped my hands into my pockets, before walking toward the terrace doors. Wynn passed Piper off to Allister before making his way behind me. He'd stop and chat with a few people first before joining me. We didn't want anyone to get suspicious. It would have been perfect if Valentine had started a fight with one of the other guests like he usually did, but it seemed that tonight Valentine was on his best behavior.

I stepped out into the night air and scanned the terrace for that familiar back. I frowned. He wasn't there. Walking farther out onto the terrace, I scanned the area for him, but didn't see him or the glow of his cigarette anywhere.

"Looking for me."

I forced myself to not react as his form appeared behind me. I slowly turned around to face him. "I thought we could have a chat." I let my lips curl up at the edges as I watched him tap the end of his cigarette. "Now, what could we talk about. Oh, I know. How about how much of a fucking bastard you are?"

Valentine's brows rose and he clutched a hand to his chest. "You wound me, brother. Are you really going to let some little human slut come between us?"

My jaw clenched and I stepped toward him, erasing some of the distance between us so I could look him in the eye. "Do not talk about Piper that way."

Grinning like a fiend, Valentine took a long drag of his cigarette before flicking his it away. "Oooh, big brother. What ever will you do about it?" He moved in until we were inches apart. "Are you going to kick my ass? Does she mean that much to you? Or is she just that good of a lay? I mean, I could see it. Her blood was oh so sweet." He put one finger after another into his mouth like he was licking off her blood right there. "Come on, give me your best shot."

Wynn appeared behind Valentine and my lips ticked up. "No, but he will."

Grabbing Valentine by the chin before he could even call out for help, Wynn snapped Valentine's neck. I searched around for anyone that might have heard us before reaching down to grab Valentine by the shoulders. "Come on, we have to get him out of here before he wakes up."

Wynn picked up Valentine's legs and we hopped over the balcony, landing in the outside gardens. "This way." Wynn jerked his head to the right of the path. "This takes it to the center of the hedge maze. It'll take forever for anyone to find him."

Not wasting any time, we hurried down the stoned path and into the tall, green hedges. Moving as quickly as we could, we almost didn't stop soon enough when we heard a giggle and then a groan. Dammit. Of course, someone would decide to fuck out here tonight.

"Wait," I told Wynn.

We listened as the sound of the two lovers moved farther away before moving once more. "It sounds like they are going to the stables."

Wynn snorted. "Fucking stables. Like he even rides them. Those beasts are too scared of his ugly mug to let him anywhere near them."

I chuckled along with him, but then quieted as we came to the center of the maze. There was a well here with a bench. Our master was a whimsical kind of vampire. It made for an odd pairing to the madness inside of him. Usually, I'd roll my eyes at his display of whimsy, but tonight I was thanking him for giving us such a convenient place to get rid of a body.

"Shit, he's waking up." Wynn shifted Valentine's legs in his arms. "I don't remember him recovering this fast before."

I scowled. "He just drained a whole woman. I should have known he'd wake up sooner rather than later." I leaned my portion of him against the bench. "Hold him."

Wynn dropped Valentine's legs and walked around the back of the bench, reaching for Valentine's arms so I could stake him. Just as Wynn touched him, Valentine's eyes flipped open and he snarled. He grabbed Wynn's hand and sank his fangs into it.

Wynn yelled and tried to pry him off of him. "Fucking stake him already. He's going to bite my fucking hand off."

I pulled the wooden stake I'd hidden up my sleeve out and rushed him. Valentine's eyes shot to me and he kicked out, hitting me in the chest. I flew back and into the nearby hedge, dropping my stake. Valentine released Wynn and grabbed the back of his head, before slamming it in the stone bench. The bench split in half and Wynn was out cold.

"You thought you could take me? With just you and the man whore?" Valentine swiped his face with the back of his hand as he climbed to his feet. "You should have brought Marcus, at least then it would be a fair fight." He picked up my discarded stake. "You know, I could forgive this if it was for a good reason, but for her? A human? Come now, brother. When did you become so weak?" he growled, then kicked me in the stomach before I could get out of the way.

I grunted and clutched the area. "I'm not weak. I just realized I didn't want to be in bed with the devil anymore."

Valentine tried to kick me again, but I grabbed his foot and twisted. He fell to the ground and dropped the stake. I scrambled over him to grab it, but his hand found it again. We struggled on the ground, each of us trying to get the upper hand.

When Valentine had me pinned to the ground, he threw his head back and laughed. "Better to be in bed with the devil than licking his boots. Now, you'll go to hell, but don't worry, I'll send your whore with you soon enough." He lifted the stake in the air, but as it came down, he was launched off of me.

Wynn tackled Valentine to the ground, his own stake in his hands. Valentine was so surprised, he didn't even realize Wynn had one as well until it was sinking into his chest cavity. Valentine made a gurgling sound in his throat, his eyes going to me. His mouth moved, but no words came out before his eyes closed and he slumped to the ground.

Sighing, Wynn wiped the blood from his forehead before looking up at me. "Well, that didn't go as planned."

"No," I agreed, dusting myself off. "It didn't."

He stood and then kicked him with his foot, but Valentine didn't move. "Now what?"

I jerked my head to the well. "We get rid of the body and get back to the ballroom before anyone suspects."

As he picked up Valentine's dead form, Wynn chuckled and murmured, "Oh, someone will suspect. They just won't be able to prove it was us."

I hoped Wynn was right. I prayed he was. But when did anything in life or death go just our way?

Chapter 20
Piper

THEY THOUGHT THEY WERE being sneaky, those silly vampires, but they weren't being sneaky at all. I knew what they were doing. They were trying to distract me.

It wasn't going to work.

Drake spun me around the floor and then dipped me. Okay, so it was working a little bit. Still, I wasn't stupid. I could see the way they were making eyes at each other and whispering. I might not be able to hear them, but I knew someone with a secret when I saw them.

Plus, there was the way Wynn and Rayne were acting earlier. Men didn't get all lovey-dovey like that unless they were planning on doing something that was going to get them in trouble. Since the only thing they could be planning was killing Valentine, I was beyond pissed.

"I know what you're doing," I murmured to Drake, as he pulled me close for a slow dance.

"Oh yeah?" Drake arched a brow, squeezing his arms around me a bit tighter. "'Cause I thought I was dancing with the hottest woman in the room."

I rolled my eyes, but grinned nonetheless. "Yes, but I know why you're dancing with me."

"Again..." His eyes slid up and down my red dress, desire clear in his gaze. "Not a mystery there."

I shook my head and smacked his chest. "No, and stop trying to distract me." Clearing my throat and getting serious, I glanced over to where the others stood off to the side. "You guys are planning something and don't want me in it."

Drake stiffened slightly, but then gave me a lopsided grin. "I don't know what you're talking about."

"Yes, you do." I gritted my teeth, and then jerked my head toward where Wynn and Antoine had reappeared. No one else might have noticed them disappearing out the terrace door just moments after Valentine, but I sure as hell did. Plus, their clothes were wrinkled. "You aren't as smooth as you guys think you are, and I'm frankly a bit hurt you wouldn't include me."

"Piper," Drake warned, shaking his head. "This isn't the place. We'll talk about it later."

Getting irritated, I pushed away from Drake. "It's always later and then later never comes. I'm tired of being treated like this." I walked away from the dance floor and toward the exit.

Stomping into the hallway, I bypassed several vampires that gave me more than a curious look. It made me slow and rethink leaving the party. Unfortunately, that gave Drake time to catch up with me. "Like what?" Drake asked, grabbing my hand. "What have we been doing that's so bad?"

I snatched my hand back and growled, "Like I'm just the help."

Just as Rayne and Allister came out of the ballroom as well, Drake stated, "You are the help."

I gaped at Drake and huffed. "Well, you pay me to clean your house. Not to fuck you, so the lot of you can go hop on a stake and be done with it."

Spinning on my heel, I marched away from them and turned a corner. Knowing it was stupid to run around a mansion full of vampires, I stopped there and listened.

Someone smacked Drake, who cried out in annoyance, and then Allister snarled, "Way to go, dumbass. I don't know how you ever get laid."

"Shouldn't we go after her?" Rayne inquired, making my heart swell. I tried to keep my thoughts clear, not wanting him to know where I was. It was bad enough he read them on accident, I didn't need him reading them when I was trying to make a statement.

It was ridiculous really. I was a grown woman and yes, they paid me to clean their house, but they didn't pay me to like them or have sex with them. And okay, so I wasn't having sex with Drake, but the point still applied. I might, probably, eventually, sleep with Drake, so if that

250

was going to happen, then he had to treat me with the respect I deserved and not like someone he could just use and keep in the dark. Especially when it came to getting retribution for myself.

"Nah, she'll be alright," Drake answered Rayne, pulling my interest. "Everyone's inside the ballroom and besides, Valentine's not going to be a problem anymore. Not for anyone."

What? Did they already do it? Was Valentine gone? A part of me was sick and elated at the same time. Sick because that meant they had killed him, and elated because, well, he was dead. He'd never terrorize me or anyone else ever again. I didn't think I would ever be so happy to hear about someone's death in my life.

Grinning from ear to ear, I stepped out from the corner intent on confronting the guys again, but they were gone. Figuring they probably went back inside the ballroom, I started back toward the doors but then stopped. Did I really want to go back in there? Could I pretend I didn't know anything? That Valentine was still going to show up at any moment? And what if there was another mind reader like Rayne in there?

No, I didn't think I could do it. This was one of the most liberating moments of my life. I couldn't keep it inside.

Pulling my lower lip into my mouth, I spun around and headed toward the kitchen. I'd surprise Antoine in his room. I was sure it was him and Wynn who had done the deed. I didn't think they liked each other enough to celebrate together, so I'd thank Antoine first, and then find Wynn and thank him. But first, I needed champagne. This was a night to rejoice and I planned on getting completely intoxicated while doing it.

Holding up my skirts, I walked through the halls and kept my eyes forward as I passed other vampires. I hoped that if they saw the bite on my neck and I didn't engage them, they'd leave me alone. Valentine hadn't been that interested in me until the others showed they were protective of me. I assumed that had more to do with their previous issues than me. I wasn't that hot of a commodity. I was sure over the years they had more than their fair share of women. I was a dime a dozen in the grand scheme of things.

"Well, aren't you precious," someone purred, before a hand grabbed my shoulder, spinning me around. Theresa stood behind me with a glass of what I assumed was blood in one hand. She had chosen another slinky gown that clung to her figure and made her boobs look great. I wasn't jealous at all. Do I sound jealous? 'Cause I'm not.

Her dark curls were pulled to the side so that most of them cascaded around her face and neck. If I wasn't sure that Wynn belonged to me, I'd be worried for our relationship. Instead, I was more worried about the way she was looking at me.

"Good evening, Theresa." I pasted on a pleasant smile. Maybe if I was nice to her, she would go away. "You look lovely. I love your dress."

Theresa arched a brow and sipped from her glass. The blood that lined the rim from where she drank made me queasy. "Really? I was rather more taken with yours. So, much color. It makes me..." Her eyes moved over my red dress and she sighed before smiling. "Hungry."

"Oh?" I glanced down at it, chuckling nervously. "The masters picked it out. I didn't think much about the color at the time. It's a bit much for what I'm used to."

Nodding in understanding, Theresa pouted her lips. "Of course not. A little peasant human like you wouldn't know the finer things in life if it bit them in their little ass. But boys sure do like to dress up their toys." She reached out and played with the lace of my sleeve. "And that's all you are, you know? A toy for them to play with and discard whenever they please."

I swallowed and lifted my chin. "I'm bound to Antoine now. It'd be a bit hard to get rid of me."

Giving a throaty laugh, Theresa gave me a pitying look as her hand wrapped around my forearm. "Oh, you poor dear. Bindings can be broken when enough pressure is applied."

I gasped as her hand squeezed my arm until I cried out. I tried to pull away, and my knees crumbed beneath me as she continued to squeeze. A sharp, agonizing pain followed by a snapping of bones had the edges of my vision darkening.

"Poor humans, so fragile. So easily broken." Her smug, smiling face was the last thing I saw before my eyes closed. "Nighty, nighty, Piper Billings."

Chapter 21
Antoine

MY EYES STAYED LOCKED on our master where he was chitchatting with one of the particularly annoying guests. He didn't seem to know anything, but that didn't mean someone hadn't told him. Our master liked to bide his time and wait for the most opportune moment to strike. Usually, when you had your pants around your ankles and your cock out.

I grimaced and took a drink of my blood. I moved it around in mouth, not liking the taste of it. There's no way this was fresh. It had to be from blood bags.

255

Old blood bags, for that matter. I guess I wasn't the favorite anymore if I didn't even deserve the good stuff.

Sighing, I placed my glass on a passing tray. Rayne and the twins came back into the ballroom without Piper. This couldn't be good.

"Where is she?" I arched a brow, searching for an explanation.

Drake scratched the back of his ear. "Well, we thought it was a good idea to let her cool off."

I laced my fingers in front of me, glancing between the three of them. "And why, pray tell, did she need to cool off?"

Allister and Rayne stared pointedly at Drake before Allister crossed his arms and scoffed, "Why don't you ask this jerkwad? It's his fault."

"What?" Drake held his hands out in front of him. "It was true. What was I supposed to say?"

"You were supposed to say, 'no, of course not, we trust you completely,' you dumbass," Rayne growled and swiped at Drake, but he ducked just in time.

I shook my head in disappointment. "This is not the time or place to be squabbling. I don't care what you said to piss her off, go find her. Just because the problem has been taken care of doesn't mean it's any safer for her. Especially right now."

Drake groaned and threw his hands up in the air. "Fine. I'll go hunt her down." He started to walk around, but then grabbed his brother by the arm. "Come on."

"Why do I have to go?" Allister complained, but followed his brother anyway. "You're the one who let her leave."

"I didn't hear you stopping her," Drake argued.

I massaged the bridge of my nose. I was immortal, impervious to sickness, and still, my brothers gave me raging migraines on a regular basis. How was that even possible?

"Where are they going?" Wynn stopped next to me, holding his own glass of blood. He'd been off making sure everyone saw him here, so we had an alibi if it came down to it.

"The dumbasses let Piper go off on her own." Rayne made a rude sound in his throat and shook his head. "They better find her before something happens to her. I'm going to be pissed if I don't get to see that sexy lingerie you fucked her in."

I arched my brow, turning to Wynn. "You had sex with Piper?"

Instead of grinning like a satisfied man, Wynn glared at Rayne. "Yes, and it was lovely."

Rayne smiled even wider, reaching out and bumping Wynn's shoulder. "Don't be coy, Wynn. Tell him how it happened. I'm sure Antoine would be thrilled to hear it."

"No," Wynn countered, pushing Rayne's hand away. "He would not. Now drop it. Before I make you."

Frowning, Rayne shrugged. "Fine. I just thought that Antoine should know who has been defiling our girl in his bed."

"You fucking cad," Wynn snarled, stepping so close to him their noses brushed. "I will end you."

I should have been surprised, but I just wasn't. It wasn't even the first time Wynn had done it. The fact that he did it with Piper, though, did make me mad. Not because they had sex, but because he used her to rub it in my face the way he did all the past lovers we'd shared.

"When Piper comes back, you need to apologize," I told Wynn, stopping his stare down with Rayne. "Disrespecting me is one thing, but you disrespected her by making your first time a pissing contest."

Rayne adjusted his suit jacket and jeered, "Yeah, what he said."

"Rayne." I warned with a sigh. "Not the time."

Wynn jerked his gaze away from Rayne and then locked it onto me. As he stared at me, his facial expression changed, and for once in his goddamned life, Wynn looked regretful. "You're right. I'm sorry. I shouldn't have done that, but in my defense..." He smirked as he stared off into the distance. "She looked so fuckable then. You're going to love it. She's wearing these thigh highs that attach to garters and her panties were—"

"Piper's gone." Drake suddenly appeared next to me with Allister. "We followed her scent until it disappeared somewhere down the hallway and couldn't find her anywhere."

"Did you check the bedrooms?" I asked, panic trying to creep in. I pushed it down and tried to remain calm in the face of so many watchful eyes.

"Yes." Allister nodded. "All of them. And the library. And the garden."

"And the drawing room. She's nowhere." Drake dragged a hand over his face and growled. "Fuck, this is my fault. I shouldn't have let her leave."

"No, you shouldn't have," I scolded, as my eyes searched the crowd for our master. When they landed on him, my blood ran cold. He met my gaze with a triumphant smirk as he lifted his wine glass full of blood in the air.

"I know who has her," I announced, before pushing through them. I stalked across the ballroom and over the dance floor until I stood before our master, Boris Stravinsky. "Where is she?"

Boris grinned and excused himself from his conversation to turn to me. "Why, I don't have any idea who you are talking about."

I growled, flashing my fangs at him, not caring who was watching. "Don't play games with me, Boris. You know damn well who I'm talking about."

His grin falter and he stepped closer to me, lowering his voice. "I'm going to excuse your rudeness because you are upset, but I will not have you disrespect me in front of all of our friends."

"They're not my friends. They're yours. Everything here is yours. You made that perfectly clear when I left your house with nothing but the clothes on my back. And it just chaps your hide that I actually made something of myself and my house without you." Anger pulsated through my veins and I found myself unable to hold back any longer. I'd been holding in so much pain and resentment, and I was tired of kissing his wrinkly old ass because he happened to have made me. Enough was enough.

"Antoine." Boris—to my annoyance—calmly patted me on the shoulder. "You clearly have some things you need to get off of your chest. Why don't we go to my study and talk about it?" He turned and then paused, gesturing his glass to the others. "And bring your brothers. Might as well get everything out in the open." To the rest of the party, he grinned and held his hands up. "Go back to the festivities, this is a family matter. I'll be back after I have a little chat with my boys."

The guests chuckled around us, which only made it all worse. He wasn't taking me seriously. He was treating me like some child he had to chastise before sending to bed without supper. I would not be patronized.

I followed Boris out of the ballroom with my brothers close on my heels. Everyone's eyes trailed after us, and I wanted nothing more than to stab them all with a stake. When we left the ballroom, Theresa waited in the hallway with Boris, looking far too pleased with herself.

"Ah, Theresa. My loyal daughter. Where have you been?" Boris stopped next to her, wrapping an arm around her waist. The way she clung to him was sickening.

Theresa leaned into Boris's touch, but her eyes were on Wynn the whole time. "Oh, just getting ready to get rid of some broken things."

"Well, the boys and I were about to have a family discussion in my study. You should join us. In fact, you should find Valentine. We might as well clear the air there as well." I forced myself not to react to the sound of Valentine's name. My brothers, I knew, weren't as skilled as I was at keeping a poker face. We had plenty of practice, but I'd had it more.

If Boris noticed, he didn't say anything, but Theresa had a sly look in her eye I didn't care for. "I already looked and couldn't find him. Maybe he got lost. Someone said they saw him head into the maze earlier."

Boris hummed. "Oh well, we'll have to carry on without him. Come."

Stiffer than before, we walked as if we were going to our own execution. Which

262

we might very well be, for all I knew. Something was going on. They were being too agreeable and secretive. I had no doubt that they took Piper, but if they knew we killed Valentine, they weren't giving it away...yet.

Entering the drawing room, my eyes instantly landed on Piper, who lay in the middle of the floor with her eyes closed. I didn't immediately rush to her, but Rayne tried to.

"Ah, ah, ah." Boris appeared between Rayne and Piper, waving his finger in front of Rayne's face. "Let's not wake her just yet. She's had quite an accident and I wouldn't want her to be in pain. Would you?"

"What did you do?" Drake growled, taking a bold step forward.

I lifted my arm to stop him from going farther. "She's not dead. You can hear her breathing. Just wait." Lifting my gaze to Boris, I calmly asked, "What do you want?"

"Why, my boys home of course." Boris laced his fingers in front of him and grinned from ear to ear. Theresa sat on the edge of his desk and watched with the amusement of a cat.

"Not going to happen." I shook my head, bearing my fangs. "Never in a million years."

"Not even for your little human?" Boris pouted. "I thought you cared for her more than that."

I stared Boris down and gritted out, "You will not touch her."

"I've already touched her." Theresa held up her hand and giggled. "And it was delicious." This time, Wynn snarled in her direction, making Theresa jump and smirk. "Oh, Wynn. Do it again. I do love when you get all riled up," she mocked, biting and clawing at him.

Boris, however, had other things on his mind. "Very well, if you won't come back to me, then perhaps you could tell me what you've done with my precious boy?"

My back stiffened. "I don't know what you mean."

Clucking his tongue, Boris shook his head. "Now who's playing games? Theresa saw you leave the ballroom after him, and then someone else saw you in the maze with him." His blood-red eyes moved over to Wynn. "Both of you. So, who did it? Who killed Valentine?"

Nobody said anything. The room was silent except for the sound of Piper's

264

heartbeat. When it was clear nobody was going to say anything, Boris sighed and lifted his arms up at his sides.

"Very well, if no one wants to confess, then I guess I'll just have to take something from you." Quick as lightning, he had Piper suspended by her throat. We all took a step toward her, but Boris warned us off. "Now, now, we don't want to go breaking something else. Breaking an arm is one thing, but a broken neck isn't something she can come back from, even with your little blood bond."

I held my hand up, making the others back down. "I did it. I killed Valentine."

Boris sighed and lowered Piper to the ground. "There we go. That wasn't so hard, now was it?" None of us relaxed, even though Piper was out of his grasp. He could easily take her and break her neck before any of us could stop him. He might not have extra powers like the rest of us, but he was faster and stronger.

"Now, what to do. What to do. How should I punish you?" Boris paced back and forth before us, drawing it out as much as he could. "Perhaps I'll have you offer up one of your brothers as my plaything." His eyes locked on to Rayne,

265

who flinched back from him, making Boris smile. "That's always a good time."

"No," I snapped. "You will not get Rayne. You will never touch Rayne again. If you want someone to play with, take me. It was me who broke code, it should be me who should be punished."

Pouting, Boris let out a bored sigh. "Now where's the fun in that? A punishment isn't really a punishment unless you can make it hurt and you, Antoine...well, we learned a long time ago that you have nothing to break. No soul. No heart. Except now..." His eyes trailed back to Piper. "It's such a pity too. She's such a pretty thing."

Drake let out a low growl but didn't move.

"No, I think I know what I want." Boris grinned, his gaze moving over to Theresa. "I need a reward for my lovely girl here and she is so partial to Wynn. I think I'll make him my gift to her."

Theresa smiled broadly, clapping her hands together. "Oh, yes please. We used to have so much fun together. Didn't we, Wynn?"

I opened my mouth to deny him once more, but Wynn cut me off. "Done."

"What?" Drake barked. "No. You can't seriously be thinking of giving into this hag."

"Hey!"

"Enough, Drake." Wynn walked over to the desk where Boris and Theresa stood. "It's done. Just get Piper out of here."

"This is stupid. Antoine." Drake grabbed my arm and shook it. "We made a promise, Antoine. Remember." He ripped open his shirt to show me his tattoo. "Blood of my brother, now and forever. Are you breaking that promise now? For her?"

I glanced down at Piper and then up at Wynn, who nodded his head. To Drake, I said, "It's Wynn's choice. Marcus, get Piper. Rayne, tell Darren to gather our things. We are cutting our visit short. We're going home."

While the others did as I asked, Allister tried to calm Drake down. I watched Wynn as he let Theresa paw all over him. Though we couldn't read each other's minds, I knew he understood the message I was trying to pass on to him. This wasn't the end. I would come back for him, and even if I had to bring the whole house down on top of us, I would bring him home.

267

Chapter 22

Piper

A HUMMING SOUND FILLED my ears as I woke up. My eyes blinked open and I checked my surroundings. I was in the bedroom Antoine and I had...I tried to push up off the bed, then cried out as a sharp pain ran through my arm and I fell back onto the mattress.

I glanced down at my arm with tears in my eyes. My right forearm was bound and splinted. I wiggled my fingers and winced.

Oh, right. That bitch Theresa broke my arm.

Carefully pushing up with my other arm, I glanced around the bedroom. I was back on the plane, which meant we'd left Boris's house of terrors. Part excited and part pissed off that they hadn't woken me so I could kick Theresa's ass, I hopped off the bed.

Someone had changed me out of the red evening gown and had put me in a slinky pair of pajamas. The way my nipples were poking through the material of the tank top told me they'd also removed my bra. My legs chilled in the short shorts, and I was tempted to put on pants, but I wanted answers first.

One step toward the door and it opened. Darren walked inside, looking even more like he had a stick up his butt than usual. He wasn't even dressed in his usual butler attire. He had jeans and a t-shirt on, and his hair was all messed up.

Frowning, I stared up at him. "What's going on? Why didn't anyone wake me? And who changed my clothes?"

Letting out an exasperated sigh, Darren shook his head. "We're going home, if that wasn't obvious enough." He moved farther into the room and I backed up until I sat down on the bed. "The masters didn't want to wake you while your arm healed. They fed you their blood while you slept, but we had to wait until we got on the plane to do it. So, it'll take a bit more time to fix it. As for who changed you, Antoine did." He knelt before me, gesturing to my arm so he could look at it.

Wincing, I lifted it so he could check the wrappings and adjust the splint. "Where'd you learn to do that?"

Darren gave me a small smile. "Before I was a butler, I was a field medic. I had to fix all kinds of injuries in the war. Well, before I got sick."

"Oh," I said, staring down at my arm as he unwrapped and rewrapped it. I was always learning new things about these guys. I wondered if I'd ever know everything. Well, I had plenty of time left to find out.

My eyes drifted over to the side of the bed where my red dress lay discarded with my lingerie. My face heated. Antoine had seen me in those garters and corset. I wondered if he liked them. It was unfortunate that he hadn't been able to take them off of me while I was conscious. Maybe I'll have to wear them again for him. Just to see what would happen.

"Is everyone else in the other room?" I asked when he was done, standing. "I'm starving, but I want to know what happened to Theresa."

"Theresa?" Darren arched a brow. "What about her?"

I lifted my arm, growling, "That bitch is the one who broke my arm. Please tell me they at least slapped her around a bit. I wasn't doing anything to her and she just up and breaks it. So rude." I huffed and held my arm close to me.

Darren shook his head, not smiling at my joke. There was something off about him. Something off about this whole thing.

"I'm sorry to say that Theresa did not get slapped around. In fact, they didn't even know she had done it." Darren sighed and turned toward the door.

My brows furrowed in confusion and I stepped closer to him. "What do you mean? How else did they find me?"

"They didn't," Darren replied, leaving the room before I could pester him for more answers.

Irritated by the non-answers, I stomped into the other room to find the guys all lounging around in their seats. They weren't laughing or playing games.

They hadn't even turned on the big screen TV. They were talking quietly until I came into the room and then suddenly, they were all silent.

What was really messed up was though I stood there scantily clad, not a single one of them ogled me or tried to hit on me. It was almost as if someone had sucked all the joy out of the room.

Getting more confused by the minute, I took a seat next to Rayne on the couch and I waited for one of them, any of them, to tell me what the hell was going on. When several minutes passed and no one offered up any information, I snapped.

"I give up. What's the joke here? What am I missing?" I scanned their faces and tried to read something in their expressions, but they were giving me nothing.

"There's no joke, babe." Rayne patted my knee with a reassuring smile. "I promise you, we aren't being dicks this time."

"Then what's going on?" I almost cried.

"What do you remember?" Antoine inquired from his chair, one leg crossed over the other as he watched me.

I slumped back onto the couch and winced as I jostled my arm. "I was dancing with Drake and you were all acting weird. A bit like now, actually, but worse. Then I told Drake that I wasn't stupid and knew you were hiding something. Then I ran out. Drake and I argued some more."

Allister snorted and Drake held his hands out in front of him in silent apology.

Not wanting to let them know that I knew they had killed Valentine, I sighed and continued, "I decided to go to the kitchen to get something to drink, but then I ran into Theresa. She said some mean stuff and then broke my arm. Next thing I know, I'm waking up here with you guys acting like somebody died."

"Valentine's dead," Antoine announced like it was no big deal. "That was what we were hiding."

"I know." I nodded and then guilty added, "I overhead Drake, Allister, and Rayne talking about it."

Rayne arched a brow.

Chewing on my lower lip, I admitted, "I was hiding around the corner, listening in."

Drake shook his head and chuckled. "Of course, you were."

"Well," I began with a huff, crossing my arms over my chest, but being careful of my broken arm. "You guys were being assholes. If I'm part of this family now, you have to trust me. Which means letting me in on the plans. You already said before it wasn't safe for me to not know stuff. Well," I held up my broken arm, "exhibit A." The masters around me at least had the decency to look guilty about it. "I'm getting tired of getting bit and beaten by your enemies because you leave me out of the loop. I hope this is a lesson to you, because I'm running out of things to break."

Antoine nodded. "Of course. You have a valid point. We will do well to include you in the future."

I nodded my head. "Good. Now, tell me how you killed Valentine."

Suddenly, it was like I'd asked Antoine to stand on his head, because everyone fell silent and became even more depressed than before. I searched for some kind of explanation but didn't find any. Even Marcus was looking more grumpy than usual.

"What?" I questioned. "What is it?"

Once more, it was Antoine who answered, "As Drake tells me, you already saw Wynn and I follow Valentine outside to the terrace. Wynn broke his neck to knock him out and then we jumped the balcony." I gasped and leaned forward, listening intently. I didn't know why I wanted a play-by-play of how they killed Valentine, but something inside of me needed to know. Like it wouldn't rest until I knew for sure that he was dead. Antoine continued on to explain how things went down, and with each word the others were becoming more and more upset. "Then we dumped his body in the well and returned to the party."

I hummed and frowned. "Why do you guys look like this is a bad thing? Valentine's dead. You're acting like he was one of your friends. Do I need to remind you that he almost killed me? That he, wait—" I jumped to my feet, my head swiveling around the room as my heart jutted against my rib cage. "Where's Wynn?"

About the Author

Erin Bedford is an otaku, recovering coffee addict, and Legend of Zelda fanatic. Her brain is so full of stories that need to be told that she must get them out or explode into a million screaming chibis. Obsessed with fairy tales and bad boys, she hasn't found a story she can't twist to match her deviant mind full of innuendos, snarky humor, and dream guys.

On the outside, she's a work from home mom and bookbinger. One the inside, she's a thirteen-year-old boy screaming to get out and tell you the pervy joke they found online. As an ex-computer programmer, she dreams of one day combining her love for writing and college credits to make the ultimate video game!

Until then, when she's not writing, Erin is devouring as many books as possible on her quest to have the biggest book gut of all time. She's written over thirty books, ranging from paranormal romance, urban fantasy, and even scifi romance.

www.erinbedford.com
Facebook.com/erinrbedford
twitter.com/erin_bedford

CPSIA information can be obtained
at www.ICGtesting.com
Printed in the USA
FSHW021528081020
74504FS

9 781951 958084